The Black Family
Towards more self-love

ESSAYS AND POETRY

By ASHER
Poetic Feelings Analyst

Our bodies survived slavery but our self-assurance did not. I urge every Black person to read these essays and poems that seek to repossess our strong feelings of self-love and seek to bring back joy and high self-esteem to the Black family.

Many say my poetry sounds like sweet music lyrics. If making music is your desire, send for written permission to the author.

Author: Asher Ledwidge

Cover design and illustration by Leroy McPherson
Typesetting by Lori Johnson

The Black Family
Published August 1993—ISBN 0-9636109-0-2
Second printing: published 2005—ISBN 0-9636109-4-5
Copyright © Asher Ledwidge 1993, 2005

All rights reserved. No part of this book may be reproduced in any form without permission in writing from the author. Printed and bound in the USA.

Send all inquiries to:
Asher, P.O. Box 120976, Clermont, Florida 34712

Acknowledgments

To Jane, my wife, thanks for loving me.

To Siri, my daughter, may she find more self-expression.

To Alex, the best brother-in-law any man can have, thanks for listening and encouraging me.

To my 3 brothers and 2 sisters, from the union of Stafford and Cassandra Ledwidge.

To my co-workers: Kenny (Chicago) Tucker, Annie Beckles and Winston George, thanks for listening and for your encouragement.

Table of Contents

Forword to the Second Printing 7
Forword 8
About Asher 9
About Black Manhood 11
Teach Me to Love 16
The Fear of Failure 17
Chain of Sorrow 18
Memories of Slavery and Grandma 19
At the Day Care 20
Blacks: Towards More Self-Love 21
How Can We Return to Self-Love? 37
Prayer for a Black Hero 42
Elijah Mohammed 43
A Letter to my Motherland 44
So They Changed Me 46
Our Nature in Common 47
Unwanted Hate 48
Thou Hath Enslaved my Soul 49
Living Black in a White World 50
Black is Beautiful 51
The Black Sees Himself 52
Black Man inside Himself 53
The Learning Defense 54
Anger—Love the Mule—the Slave 55
Equality 56
The White Man 57
Black is Equal 58
How it Feels to be Black 59

The Good, the Bad and the Me	60
Black, Get Back	62
How the White Man Sees Me	63
Black in the Mirror	64
Friendship from a Black Perspective	65
I Dump on my Kids	69
The Black Family in America	70
Love, Discipline and the Child	75
Don't touch my Glass	77
Suppress the Hurt, Embrace the Comfort	78
Can't Find a Home	80
Sad, My Dad	81
The Barber's Chair	82
Footsteps of Mama	83
Let Me Drink	84
Positive Thinking	85
Empty Bottle, Empty Room	86
Confession of a Junkie	87
The Last Day of my Life	88
Knowing that You Love Me	89
A Duet for Happiness	90
MLK, Jr., Compassion and Wisdom	91
Lord, Forgive our Unbelief	92
Lord, My Spirit Looks up to Thee	93
A Black Anthem	94
Give a Child Love	95
Being Black and Male	97

Foreword to the Second Printing

When an author writes a new foreword to a book that was published 11 years ago, the first question he asks himself is whether he will want to correct the text of any essential points he now considers to be erroneous. Since my ideas and my life have changed and developed during those years, I was quite prepared in reading the book to find a number of statements I might like to change. To my surprise, I found no need for change, and I have decided to reprint the book the same as it stood 11 years ago.

Except to say, today I live in Florida with a new wife of three years, and I have a brighter attitude about life, love and the pursuit of happiness. Also, today I have published a total of four books and will soon publish my next book, *The Soul of the Black Culture*. In 1993 when I wrote this book I did not know how **right** I was in saying self-love provides the very foundation and roots of a loving family.

So today in the year 2004, my message remains the same as it was 11 years ago. We need to put the integrity of Black families first, that's putting self-love first.

Asher 2004

The Black Family

Foreword

I recently had a joyful experience. Over lunch an old friend of mine, Asher Ledwidge, introduced me to a collection of his personal poetry. Poems such as "The Fear of Failure," "Expressing His Grief," "Joy and the Polarity of Feelings" leaped out at me and endeared their messages into my soul.

The uniqueness of Asher's poetic work is in how he is able to integrate real life axioms into wondrous works of rhymes, rhythms and poetic expressions that combine to break down the complexities of life into the innocence of our first lessons in life.

This is how in "Expressing His Grief" (a poem Asher wrote for me), he is able to teach us a noble lesson. Through the use of homespun axioms and poetic expressions, Asher makes this statement: "He takes a lesson from the infant child, who learned to cry before he learned to smile."

The beauty of homespun axioms is three fold. Homespun axioms are politically correct, gender neutral and sometimes in literature, a small dose of reality is worth a ton of rhetoric.

Thank you, Asher, for not taking out a literary license to engulf society in another caricature approach to realism. It is a relief to find a writer who did not stumble down from the mountain top to lecture us on the society we live in.

Finally, I have a quotable literary figure to strengthen my soul, without having to read through chapters of rhetoric.

Kenneth Tucker

Self-Love or Self-Destruction

The Black Family

About Asher

I was born a black baby on May 3, 1941 in Jamaica, West Indies. I was one of six children of an unhappy marriage. My father was a butcher who also cultivated bananas and coconuts. Mother had a small garden and made oil from coconuts to sell.

Mother's personality, which most influenced my life, contained the ultimate good and evil you could find in one person. On one hand a good and caring person, but with a very fiery temper. She would knock me down on the floor just for talking back to her.

My consuming passion as a child was to grow up, get rich and famous so I could find someone (some woman) who looked like my mother, to love me.

I engaged in a constant search for happiness to relieve the sorrow of a loveless childhood.

At 18, I went to live in Kingston with my aunt. I worked as an apprentice electrician. I was always obsessed with studying and learning, believing that knowledge would make me important (so that I could get a pretty girl to love me).

I came to New York City in February 1964 on a student visa, to work and study. I went to the RCA Institute; and at NYCC I took further courses in electrical engineering.

My early years in NYC were very, very troublesome. I found no happiness, no peace of mind, no pretty girl to love me. I became very sick and went to the doctor about twice a week. The doctor said, "Son, I can't really find anything wrong with you, I'll have to send you to a psychiatrist." This was in 1965. I began therapy twice a week at Kings County Hospital, Brooklyn.

The Black Family

My activity consisted of working in factories as an electrician. For a spiritual uplifting I sang in the church choir. Working, studying, therapy and chasing girls consumed the rest of my time.

Some time about 1968 I stopped therapy. I got married in 1970; finding marriage difficult to cope with, forced me back to therapy. Most of the 1970s I was going to therapy trying to relieve my stress and anxiety. Much anxiety.

My first real breakthrough was when I met David Bricker, Ph. D. I started studying with him once a week. With him therapy was not just sitting and talking; I began to explore my innermost feelings and to read books on feelings that Dr. Bricker recommended. I became associated with the Institute for Rational Living and began to work on my anger by rational behavior therapy. Anger was something I could not previously feel. I continued studying at RBT until about 1989. This entailed extensive exercises in the RBT techniques.

One Saturday while watching channel 13, I saw John Bradshaw speak about Homecoming, bringing home the sad and lonesome child in all of us. This was right up my alley, so I bought all of Bradshaw's books and tapes.

Today I am divorced from my first wife (one daughter Siri), remarried and much happier. I became a member of the International Institute of Bioenergetics.

Bioenergetics is a new type of psychoanalysis. It was founded by Alexander Lowen, M. D. who has 40 years of experience as a therapist. Of the 12 books he has written, I have the privilege of saying that I've read 11 of them.

The basic premise of bioenergetic therapy is that unity means emotional harmony; disunity (or emotional splitting) results in emotional disturbance. This has changed my life mostly in the area of self-expression: Joy, Sorrow, Fear and Anger. One of the most important things about me today is the way I look at the world and at other people, as feeling human beings rather than as products of material success. An example: a

The Black Family

millionaire who goes home to an alienated family in a loveless home might be considered less successful than a floor sweeper who provides for a family that loves and respects him.

What can be concluded from my past? I was a boy who grew up very weak, very, very angry without the ability to express this anger. A boy whose fear of being frightened was an everyday horror.

Throughout a constant economic struggle to succeed by electrical technology, buying and selling houses, a passion for investing in stocks (bonds and mutual funds), deepest and strongest passion was to ease my agony and find some pleasure in life through psychotherapy: a constant analysis of my feelings so as to understand Asher and why Asher feels the way he does about himself and about the world around him.

I believe I had joyful success in all the above and today have more self-expression than I ever thought possible. Still, every time I see a pretty girl I like, my affection starts to bubble, but anxiety steps in because of the fear she might turn me down, making me feel I'm no good.

About Black Manhood

One Sunday in September 1992, I went to a church in St. Albans. It was "Men's Day" at the church. The speaker was brother Rev. Al Sharpton. Before the speech my expectation was low: I thought he was going to talk about discrimination and the white man. To my happy surprise, his topic was one thing only: MANHOOD.

He said:
- Being a male and being a man can be two different things.
- Men don't let kids take over their neighborhood with drugs.
- Men take care of their babies and go to the schools to see what their kids are learning.
- Men work to better their communities.
- Big house, big car, big coat is not a show of manhood. Even a Ph. D. does not show manhood. Manhood is a **feeling**, not an **image**!

I believe the Rev.'s speech changed my life. Most of all it put a heavy pressure on my conscience. It left me with guilt. I considered myself a

Self-Love or Self-Destruction

The Black Family

happy, blessed black man, but I am not doing anything to help those less fortunate than myself.

How many black males only see a need for black activity when it comes to a personal confrontation about a racial issue? As long as his own thing is going smoothly, he stays wrapped up in himself.

As a young man searching for love:
- Every man I saw I was afraid of, afraid he was going to beat me up; whether he was 100 or 300 lbs. (while I was 200 lbs).
- I was obsessed with learning: If I look smart and have a degree, I'll get love and acquire importance.
- Most of my life, in my sorrow and loneliness, nobody cared about me. All I needed (I felt) to be happy was for an important woman to love me. I'm working as hard as I can to be good enough to make her love me.
- For a long time I wanted to get my electrical license and to have my own business. But each time I made a move towards that goal, I got so nervous I had to back off.
- If I get money to buy enough glamorous things, I'll get someone to love me and I'll be happy.
- Every time I see a man carrying a briefcase or a suit on, I say he must be happy, and I'd like to be like him. How come I cannot be like him and be happy?
- Each time I see a pretty girl I like, affection and anxiety conflict; I always feel afraid she might turn me down.
- Deep fear and anxiety that I was going to get sick. If I ever get sick, I'm so unimportant that nobody will care for me.
- If I'm not doing anything to improve my social importance like making money or studying, I begin to feel useless and hopeless. I need a degree to feel important.
- I must find a girl to love me, to hug me.
- I could not feel anger as a youth.
- After eight years of therapy, I began to feel it a little.

Self-Love or Self-Destruction

The Black Family

- Feeling anger: At first I felt like I was going insane.
- Being investing in the stock market from 1972.

Things I always counted on for happiness that failed:
- Making money.
- A job wearing a suit and tie.
- Boss on the job.
- Having a pretty, important girl to love me.
- Plastic surgery on my nose.
- Electrical engineering degree.
- Publish a book.
- The white man on the job having me sitting beside him in the office.
- Trying to please every man, woman and child so they will love me.
- Panic and anxiety on seeing a light-skinned woman; needing her to love me.
- Having many, many good ideas in my life but the fear of success caused me to run away from them.
- The thing I wanted most, a good woman, I feared the most!
- I had to smile at everybody.
- If I don't smile they might think I'm mad at them.
- Never been broke after earning my first penny.
- Could have made boss on the job, but was afraid to.
- At about 25 years old, a white man hollered at me. I got sick and trembled.

A little black boy from a little town in Jamaica could never be important.

My early days on the job I had friendly relationships with two white fellows. We had good work times and even socialized (went to movies) out of work. One day I had a disagreement with both of them and thought they were angry with me. We were no longer so chummy. The feeling of these two boys not talking to me was unbearable. The way I saw it at the time, the only reason I was unhappy was that I, Asher, was not important,

Self-Love or Self-Destruction

was a nobody. My one desire was to make up with them, so I wouldn't have to continue feeling this way. It was a sad day in my life.

Some Positive Changes in my Life

The most important positive change for me today regards the way I see people (which is a reflection of how I see Asher).

I spent most of my life either looking down at people or up to them (a man with money or a big education I'd have to look up to).

A man who cannot read or who swept floors, I looked down on (but they might possess great spirituality)! This looking up or down at people causes a whole lot of anxiety. You find no peace therein.

The positive change today is that I don't look at people, I look through them. This affords peace of mind. You look at people's expression, sad or joyful.

I can see a millionaire crying in sorrow and I pity him; a Ph. D. who has no self-expression, I would say is a sad person; one with a lot of self-expression, I would feel good about because he probably has some joy.

If I see a man sweeping a floor, I don't look at the broom in his hand, but at his face; or speak with him to discover his joy or sorrow (is he a loving man with a wife and kids who love him, and so on?).

My Dreams

When I was young, all my dreams were haunted; they contained a lot of sorrow and pain; Someone or something was always capitalizing on my weakness.

Today I find self-expression in my dreams; I remember them more. Sometimes I have two or three dreams a night: about my mother and father. I can get angry in these dreams and express my anger. What a relief!

Money. I no longer see money as the key to my happiness. I have enough money today to fulfill my basic needs for now and for the future. I guess what this means is that fulfilling my need is the key to my happiness, fulfilling my greed is not! Also, very important, I no longer think that for me to find a lot of love, money is the answer. A lot of poor people have love and are happy.

Emotional happiness is self-expression, self-control and self-awareness. To love and to be loved is the key to happiness.

Today I'm the proud author of over 350 poems all about human emotions; about pain and pleasure, inspired by the writings of some great psychologists like Alexander Lowen, Wilhelm Reich (a student of Freud who went deeper than Freud); and by a Muslim psychologist named Dr. Akbar, I will continue my quest for happiness, for more self-expression, for more self-love.

Thank you!

The Black Family

Teach Me to Love

*T*he dream of a little child is to be playful, naughty and wild
I am ready, willing and able to give you all my smile.

My father, uncles, brothers, seem so far away.
Come get me Mama,
Come love me Mama,
Will I make it through the day?

Will I be lonely? Will I be loved?
Hugging, kissing, give me the things there cannot be too much of.
Teach me how to love myself so I can love you back each day.

Is this a lonely house without love?
With no people for me to play?
Can I be loved in this house, or do I have to run away?

Come and get me Mama,
Embrace me, lift me high up to the sky.
I want you, I need you, Mama.
Teach me how to love myself.
Love me or I'll die.

Note: This is the first poem I wrote. It caused me to cry many times.
-- ASHER

Self-Love or Self-Destruction

The Fear of Failure

Of all the feelings that rattle my soul,
The fear of failure
Is the one that most often knocks me cold.

Many, many times I've failed in the past,
It wasn't that terrible
No one nailed me to the cross.

Most of the time my little elf,
There's nothing to fear but fear itself.

It seems it's the fear of feeling the fear,
If I feel fear I'll fail.

If the actual failing is the coffin,
Then feeling the fear is the nail.

Be it riding an elevator or taking a test
For me to feel like I'm failing,
Like I'm falling, it's a mess.

Since the coat of the fear of failure
And my chance for success
Are hanging in the same sack,
How can I be sure which one is causing my anxiety
When I step up to the rack?

The Black Family

Chain of Sorrow

They say the sins of the parents shall pass from generation to generation.
Black people for over 400 years
Have suffered great exploitation.

The sorrow and pain from slavery days is the longest chain in the world,
The chain links from generation to generation,
Down to every boy and girl.

Unlike a chain of steel that can rot and decay,
A chain of sorrow can last one million years
'Cause it just gets longer and longer each day

To stop the chain of sorrow from grow
We must change the seeds we are sow.
Seeds of kindness, seeds of love, throughout our community.
We must sow seeds of love and respect within the family.

Chains of sorrow have been broken
From my neck, my ankle,
But there is still the chain on my soul that's a fact.
Each day and night I still have to fight
To get this monkey off my back.

Self-Love or Self-Destruction

The Black Family

Memories of Slavery and Grandma

I often sit and wonder what if my great grandmother from slavery was around today.
As she looked at my sorrow and pain what would she cry her heart out and say?

Would she be sorry for the torch of anger, fear and insecurity that she passed down to me?
Would she say how she tried hard to love me but the demons would not let her be?

Would she tell about her ancestors back there in Africa land?
How lots of love and respect for self and community was always on hand?

Would she explain how we were a happy people, and how our love was lost?
Lost with each crack of a whip and each time she said "yes sa massa boss."

I am going to teach my children how to love again,
I'll teach them how to break the chains of violence, sorrow and pain.

So dear old Grandma, in your grave,
Don't you weep too much for me, 'cause as sure as there's a God above,
I'm going to set myself free.

With me, memories of you, and the spirit of God above,
I'm going to try my very best
To teach me how to love.

Self-Love or Self-Destruction

The Black Family

At the Day Care

*I*s this the day care center I'm at?
How can she care for me.
There're too many kids in here.

What I need right now is a soft and tender lap to sit.
They just leave me sitting on the floor.
I need for them to feed me,
It's too many kids coming through the front door.

From this day care with so little care,
Mommie take me home at nights,
I want to hug her but she seems not to be there.

Nobody to read me my story book
After my prayer is said.
I'm lonely with the TV
In a dark room in my bed.

The Black Family

BLACKS:
Towards More Self-Love

Self-love, what is it? Why do I believe we Blacks in the western world have lost our self-love and will be in big trouble if we do not work towards loving ourselves more?

Ask anyone, "Do you love yourself?" He will say, "Yes, I do. How could I not love me?" To some degree every person alive has some self-love. A total loss of self-love would mean death. So we must talk about the quantity of self-love. How much do I love myself?

It is my strong belief that as a people, we Blacks have less love for ourselves than the rest of the people. I came to this belief not by asking, but by observing the way we act. The way we treat ourselves and the other Blacks in our community, without respect.

In the following pages I will briefly explain:
- How we first possessed self-love.
- How we lost it.
- How we can work towards more self-love

A child came into this world. He was born with a very, very strong instinct to love and be loved. The child's normal instinct to love will move towards his parents, his mother and father or any care giver. These people will be his love object.

The child's need to be loved is the most important thing to him. To him it is a matter of life and death.

Every healthy infant is born with the enormous ability to love and be loved. He wants to give all his love and desperately wants to believe that his parents love him.

Being born into this world is a very traumatic experience filled with a lot of uncertainties and anxieties. It's easy to understand the child's being frightened, knowing that he cannot survive without someone to

Self-Love or Self-Destruction

The Black Family

take care of him. So he needs a lot of love and assurance from the adults, a lot of love and attention from them. The child must know that he will be loved, he will be taken care of. If the parents do not act in such a way, loving him, giving the infant this assurance, terrible things will happen.

Without the love that brings assurance and acceptance, the infant develops all kinds of neurotic symptoms like anxiety, anger, hate, feelings of abandonment, feelings of inferiority. The child at first will try to express all these negative feelings towards the parents who should love him but could not. Then an even greater dilemma comes upon the child when he discovers he cannot successfully hate his care-givers because that is even more frightening because he will lose the hope of ever getting taken care of and that would mean he would die.

So what happens? The child is left with one choice, to turn the hate around to himself, resulting in his loss of self-love. No love, no self-love.

Another big dilemma for the child is that he cannot consciously hate himself either so he puts this information in the back of his head in the unconscious, and continues to openly believe he is still in love with himself.

Now if this child lives to be 100 years old, he always will be emotionally very weak because of the loss of love. He will be a man who is unable to remember when he lost his self-love because his infantile mind could not comprehend all that went down at the time. Admitting that his self-love is lost is very frightening, with feelings of abandonment. He has to wake up each day and try telling himself he has love but needs more.

The one thing that his loveless parents could not take away from him was his hope, so hope keeps him going, and human spirit. He will spend the rest of his life looking for love, hoping to find someone who will love him. He will go through pain and sorrow to find this love because without it he'll feel like he is nobody. He desperately needs love. He will feel as he did as an infant: "I am not good enough for anyone to love me. I am a nobody, not good enough."

Self-Love or Self-Destruction

The Black Family

Destructive type behavior is typical of people with little self-love or even self-hate. This is typical of people who drink too much, eat too much, work too much, take drugs, and are always hurting other people—even someone who tries to love them. And, all the time blaming other people for their unhappiness. Blaming them for not loving him.

The Black Experience: Diminishing of Self-Love

Back in the West Coast of Africa (where we came from), before the slave trade began, we were a happy people. A people with great ability to love and be loved.

Love started with the infant child. This child became very important in the family for about the first two or three years of his life. He was number one!

The family unit was such that the needs of this infant were most important. Mothers did not leave their babies. In the families of that time it was not always the mother and father who were responsible for the care of the child. In some families the biological father of the child was not part of the family so the mother's father, uncle, or brothers would provide the father-image for the child. (Or male-image, you could say.)

The family unit was very strong. Love and respect for each other within the unit was very strong and a new born child would surely receive all the love and attention that's necessary for a healthy emotional development.

The reader might ask how they could be happy when they lived a primitive existence—no big cars, no big houses, no fur coats, no diamonds or gold chains, no Ph. D. in physics. Well, there is plenty of evidence to show that they were happy. They were happy because they believed in being themselves. They knew the secret of happiness which is to love and be loved, and to be one with their environment, one with nature. They were not oppressed. Nobody gave them a false promise of happiness with big cars and money. They did not burn with jealousy because the

The Black Family

neighbors had a bigger car. Happiness was hunting, fishing, with love of the self and love for each other.

Self-love is the foundation for happiness.

Slavery was a very cruel and inhumane experience. It took a human away from the most important thing in his life—his family—and put him in chains, robbed him of his freedom, robbed him of his self.

For many of the captured this was a fate worse than death. Death would be a welcome relief, as shown by the fact that many of them killed themselves.

The beginning of this experience is the beginning of the sad lesson on how to stop loving oneself.

The capturing of a human and the taking away of his freedom causes him to be very angry. Anger soon turns to fear and anxiety when he is unable to remove the chains of his oppressor. The anger, fear, anxiety, rage stay with him. It is very painful to consciously harbor these negative feelings because they put a heavy burden on his sanity. Resist as he will, he soon will get tired and give in to his oppressor.

Giving in to brutality and oppression is a very complicated phenomena, especially when the hate runs very deep when he is being chained and beaten.

As long as the anger in him is conscious, he'll have the urge to act, to take flight or fight, either of which he cannot do. So the reverse psychology steps in. The slow process of looking at the oppressor with a little less hate each day. If the reverse psychology really works well, you might even get to like this man with the whip and chains. After all, he feeds you, keeps you alive. Where there is life, there is hope. But believe me brothers and sisters, the anger and hate do not go away, but are deeply suppressed in your body—in your stomach and chest—causing much pain and discomfort. But you become less frightened because you really do not hate anybody, so the danger of killing or being killed is happily removed. At the same time though that you have stopped hating the oppressor, unknowingly or unconsciously, there are some people who you can hate without being put in any danger. And the first in line for this

Self-Love or Self-Destruction

The Black Family

hate is **thyself**, and also the brothers and sisters in chains. They will not hurt you. They do not have anything against you. They are harmless. Loss of love for brothers! This experience is the most tragic thing that could happen to you. Love for the oppressor, and an equal loss of love of the self.

Loss of self-love is also a terrible feeling but it is bearable and even becomes acceptable after you find some excuses for why you feel so bad, why this terrible thing happened to you. Excuses like "maybe it's because something is wrong with me!" Or, "look, my skin is black; I am primitive; God made me weak; God put a curse on me; I am not as good as the oppressor; I hope one day I'll be good again, one day before I die!" Maybe he **will** die.

Living with Loss of Self-Love

Each day you awaken with an emptiness inside of you; sadness, loneliness, fear, anxiety. You are heartbroken. Each day is a struggle to fill the void inside of you. Dancing, singing, eating, drinking, will not fill the emptiness inside, but they always help temporarily to remove the hurt so you can feel better.

But feeling better times are few and far between because each day the experience of slavery puts a burden on your self-love. When the Massa rapes your wife or daughter in front of you and you cannot kick his ass or kill him you just have to grin and bear it. That anger and hate for him is turned on yourself, eating away at your self-love. Pity and sorrow are the only things you can feel. The anger must be quickly suppressed or your life will be in danger. Danger because anger will urge you to strike back and get killed.

Remember, we said the family unit was one of the most important things our ancestors had back in Africa. The family unit was very strong with a whole lot of self-love, a whole lot of love for each other, and a whole lot of love and respect for the community and for nature. Believe me, with all that love they did not have to wake up each morning searching desperately for love. And since only love can bring happiness, they were

Self-Love or Self-Destruction

The Black Family

happy. No need to seek happiness in big cars, big houses, fur coats, social achievements. These things will add to happiness but the foundation for happiness must be self-love. When you love yourself you are free to love your fellowman and your community.

The oppressor was very smart in his cruel oppression. He knew for sure that he could be successful in taking away our self-esteem and replacing it with bottled-up anger and fear. We would stop resisting his brutal treatment and become obedient to him. He could oppress us and get our respect and obedience at the same time. How fortunate he was. He could get the same thing out of us that he got from a donkey just by breaking him in.

So he split our families apart. He found that to be very effective. Motherhood, fatherhood, brotherhood, sisterhood, unclehood, grandmotherhood, were no more to be cherished. The oppressor would take the place of all these with ultimate control.

So we were put out to breed, just like animals. Just have sex, have babies, with no need to give a damn about them. Don't worry. They don't need love. We do not care about strong character or emotional health, just strong backs.

Black men did not feel any shame in fathering a child and walking away from bringing up that child. His responsibility is to go father another one. Just get all the sex you can get. No time or necessity to be a father or an uncle or a brother.

Then the mother is so burned up with anger and sorrow that it's next to impossible to raise an emotionally healthy child. The child will grow up with great fear and sorrow and anger. The male child will not know what real manhood is. He lost his manhood. He has a lot of regret because he is trying so hard to be a real man but each day it seems his manhood is slipping away from him. He has to find negative, self-destructive behaviors to get a little feeling as a man. His clothes, his car, his woman, all gave him a little macho manhood, not realizing his manhood was lost back in slavery. He forgot he had to abandon his true self and his manhood in order to survive the oppression of slavery.

Self-Love or Self-Destruction

The Black Family

Loss of Self-Love after Slavery 'till Today

After slavery was abolished and the physical chains removed, we went on wrongly to believe that we were free. We were anything but free. The mold was set and dry. The making of a people immersed in sorrow, anger, and great fear was completed. What was done could not be undone by removing anything physically.

The castration of a people, once begun, will continue from generation to generation until a conscious effort is made on the part of that people to reverse the process.

There is much evidence around today to show that Blacks are still psychologically slaves. But we are not enslaved by another person right now in 1992. We enslave ourselves through oppression of our minds. We are enslaved by the destruction of broken families. We are enslaved by the loss of love and respect for our ourselves, our brothers, and our community. We are enslaved by the lack of communication between us. We are enslaved by parents with low self-esteem who bring up kids without love or self-esteem. We are enslaved by the false promises the oppressor gave us, as to what happiness is, by our false image of happiness. We are enslaved by still having more respect for the oppressor than we have for ourselves. We are enslaved by drugs, alcohol, lust, and loss of direction, by violence perpetuated on each other, violence even between family members.

The hate-anger-fear that slavery put upon us is with us today as it was 300 years ago, turning on the self and destroying the self each and every day. We are in big trouble! Trouble because nobody can save us. Nobody can save us from ourselves.

The oppressor is not going to give us back our self-love. He has nothing to gain by it.

The task ahead of us is to get out of psychological slavery, restore ourselves to emotional strength, and find ourselves again.

Our ship of self-love is drifting, drifting in the sea of anger-hate-fear-rage. We are in an ocean of self-destruction. We must change course to get back, to find our true selves, to find our identity, our individuality. To find joy, peace, love and happiness.

What is Self-Love?

I was forced into this explanation by my daughter. When I told her I was writing about self-love she said, "You talk about yourself too much."

I told her my writing is not about just me, but about me, you, and the whole Black race of people in the western part of the world. Blacks in America, Jamaica, Trinidad, South America. It's about a group of people who were brought from Africa to be slaves.

Then she said, "Oh, I understand. But I think you're wrong, Daddy. I do not think we need self-love. I think we love ourselves too much."

I must explain. Self-love, or the love of one's self, is something very, very few people—black or white—have a lot of. Very, very few have a good understanding of what self-love is and what it is all about.

The first thing to understand is that self-love and happiness go hand in hand. We must first love ourselves before we can love another. The need for love and happiness is the most important thing for any human to seek after. There is no such thing as too much love.

If there is no such thing as too much self-love, then why did my daughter say we love ourselves too much? Is it because she is foolish? No. Far from it.

I would say that her definition of self-love, or even love, is wrong.

Examples: When one says, "I am going out and buy me a $500 coat. I am going to treat myself good," that's not self-love because all our body really needs is a coat to keep it warm (say for about $100). That's love of the image of himself. The coat will bring up his image to a level where he can love and all the people around him will love. The love of an image, but not the self. Just an image of the self. He can look in the mirror and love himself.

When a man or woman claims to love himself or herself and eats the best steak and drinks the best wine until they get too fat and get sick,

The Black Family

that's not love. That's too much self. That's loving the food and wine at the expense of the self, at the expense of the body, because your body is yourself, and an unhealthy mind creates a distorted image of yourself. The love of the self is lost.

But, not to worry. I have something to hold on to. This lovable image of myself.

So what we have is a man with his true self. His true identity is lost. He struggles each day to find out who he is and where he fits in the human race, who is going to love and understand him. A lot of questions but no answers because he must first love and understand himself. All he is doing is loving what he thinks is himself.

So it's Okay to Love the Image

Let's say being in love with an image is not the worst thing that can happen to a man, because without some kind of love or hope for some kind of love, it would be very difficult to stay alive. So it's okay to love the image.

Let's call love of your body love of the true self. All other love is distorted love. Distorted love is seen everyday around us. Most forms of extreme behavior can be attributed to distorted love or lack of self-love.

Extreme jealousy in the name of love. Extreme kindness in the name of love. But giving in order to control, like parents sometimes do with kids. These are forms of distorted love.

Extreme obedience—be it to your wife, husband, friend or lover—in the name of love. No, that's not love, but a lack of self-love and an attempt to get love through obedience.

Extreme show of love to any and everybody, never being able to say no or openly refuse anyone, is distorted love and a lack of true self-love.

Extreme anger or inability to get angry is a lack of self-love. So is pushing oneself to achieve each and every goal, to be the best at everything, and to be perfect all the time.

Loss of Self-Love

Extreme laziness and no desire to do anything is lack of self-love. Sitting around wanting someone else to take care of you is a lack of self-love.

What is commonly known as low self-esteem or a feeling of insecurity is caused by a lack of self-love.

At the bookstore I saw a book titled *Women Who Love Too Much*. True love cannot be too much. Distorted love can be too much. An adult begging helplessly for love, in deep desperation to love, has an inadequate amount of self-love.

As a matter of fact, every type of human behavior has its roots in the halls of self-love or lack of it thereof. It is self-love, the ability to love and be loved, that keeps us alive.

When we are in love or believe someone loves us, or when we love someone or love God, we feel joy and pleasure. We feel at one with ourselves, at one with our environment. Simply put, we feel good.

A lack of love or no love gives us the opposite feelings that we call negative feelings. Sadness, loneliness, self-pity, anger, and even hopelessness.

The Ability to Love

True love must be a two-way street. People who seek love on a one-way street will not find true love. If they are lucky they can find what I call distorted love. Distorted love is better than no love at all.

The expression of love must be to love and be loved. It's the exchange of pleasure between two people that brings the joy of love, or between two bodies.

The Enemies of Love

The enemies of love are suppressed anger, fear, and very important, distrust. All the above Blacks have plenty of. Trust me, we have!

The Black Family

The core or foundation of love lies deep in our hearts from the day we are born. If fear takes over, we become frightened to love and build bricks around our heart. Mistrust is the feeling of: if I give my heart to you, will you handle it with care? Will you always treat me tenderly and in every way be fair? I am afraid I'll be hurt again. This is distrust as the song says.

Being frightened or unable to trust are the policemen or guards that block feelings of love from entering or leaving the heart. So in order to love and be loved the blanket of fear and mistrust must first be resolved internally. We can learn how to trust our fellow human.

When the blanket of fear and mistrust is removed, we come upon a deep and strong wall of suppressed anger. Then we must work to resolve the suppressed anger and find positive ways of expressing it without causing any danger to our welfare, to ourselves. As we start to get in touch with the policemen, self-communicator, and get to the great walls of suppressed anger to feel and express the anger in a positive way. No violence.

Most people believe that anger and violence go hand in hand. I say no. Anger is just a feeling. If it's bottled up too much it can and will cause rage or violence. But we sure can feel anger and just feel it without any physical act to compensate.

Every one of us has had a time in our life when we felt anger without any physical act following, just some heavy breathing.

If we can resolve those outer layers of fear and mistrust and some suppressed anger, the light of day will shine into our hearts and love will come in.

There are people out there who know how to love and be loved. They can speak of the joy and happiness that love brings.

Love is accepting the joy from a one-year-old boy as he smiles when he sees you coming, and not get angry and beat him up later when he is crying and crying. Love is lifting up a six-year-old boy or girl, hugging and kissing them, telling them you love them, and watching them smile.

Watching them trying as hard as they can to love you back and hug you back.

Love also is a 15-year-old girl sitting in class, seeing a 15-year-old boy walk in, and as she looks at him, chills run up and down her spine. Love is a feeling of just wanting to be close and not having to go to bed with another person.

To love and be loved is the greatest gift God gave to man. Let us go back to God, go back and learn how to love.

God gave us the gift of love but we messed up. We are telling God, "Who cares about love? What we need is more technology, more money, and more big machines."

Of all the animals, man is the biggest fool. Fools forget that love is what we came here for. Fools forget that love of self and our fellowman is the only thing that can save us from self.

The hard choice is self-love or self-destruction.

Can We be Emotionally Whole Again?

Can we return to self-love, to the state we enjoyed before we were captured and robbed of ourselves? Robbed of who we were before the oppressor took our love and taught us how to hate, how to be self-destructive.

I say we can, but it is not easy. It is not easy because of the nature of man. The nature of man is to adapt to most any kind of suffering and use perverted ways to convince ourselves that we are okay, that there is nothing wrong, nothing needs fixing. Even if something is wrong, there's nothing I as one person can do about it. It's not my fault anyway. If I can find someone to blame for my dilemma, it convinces me that I can do nothing about it so I might as well stay as I am today. I am okay.

So, can we be whole again? Yes, we can. But how to get us to believe that something is wrong? How to get us to stop looking towards the oppressor to save us with handouts and government programs? How to get us to understand that our hunger for love is just as strong as our hunger for food? How to get us to understand that the love of the self is the most

The Black Family

important possession a human can have? How to truly define self-love? How to get us to understand that self-love is not about just things money can buy. How to get us to understand that if a man should gain the world and lose his soul (lose his love) he is nothing. And, most of all, how do we get to understand the truth about self-love, about the ecstasy of love and the agony of hate.

If we can come to the tough conclusion about who we are, what we need, about our emotion inferiority. If we can accept these things we can be whole again. We can learn to love again. If we can accept the unpleasant truth about ourselves, the truth that only us can save us. The white man cannot and will not save us. If we stop blaming and start reclaiming our self-love, we will be whole again.

Denial and Blaming

Denial and blaming has its place in the human mind. Whenever we have bad feelings and feel helpless or unable to do anything about them, they make us feel even worse. So denial and blaming serves as a temporary relief to make us feel a little bit better.

Example of blame and denial. One day as I was leaving my house, my wife said to me, "Ash, take off that shirt. It's dirty."

Without even thinking, I quickly said to her, "It's not dirty. I have to go."

But the further I got from the house, the more the question kept haunting me. Is this shirt dirty? Do I have to go back and take it off? I sure do not feel like going back.

At this point I did not even look at the shirt to see if it was really dirty (denial), because I subconsciously knew within my heart that if I became convinced the shirt was dirty, I would feel nothing but bad about wearing a dirty shirt. Who needs to feel bad? Nobody.

A short time went by. I could not avoid feeling self-conscious about this shirt. Is it or is it not dirty? So I had to look at it. And, you guessed it,

Self-Love or Self-Destruction

The Black Family

the shirt **was** dirty. I needed to change it. But a change at that point was very difficult. I was too far away from home.

At last I started thinking, it's her fault. She should have washed my shirt. She did not, and now come to tell me the shirt was dirty!

She is a lazy woman!

I don't need her to tell me anything! (BLAME!)

So with the denial first and blame after, I was able to successfully remove the demons of guilt and shame from my feelings.

I have learned how to feel good wearing a dirty shirt. The tools of denial and blaming served me well. I was on my way to a better day.

<u>Denial of our lost love and blame the white man.</u> The example about the shirt is used to simplify the problem. When we're possessed by the demons of self-hate, anger, rage, fear, we are in a far greater dilemma than just a dirty shirt. But denial and blaming serves in the same way to get us through each day.

But in the midnight hour, these demons will raise up from the grave, from the pit of your stomach, and you'll feel heartburn. You will feel like a little man with a torch in your belly. You'll feel like your eyes, your ears, your lips, your neck are all tense and tight, and your soul is crying out for help. Where is the light? When will it be daybreak so I can see the sun again?

In the middle of the night, when denial and blaming turn to sorrow and shame and those demons keep knocking at the door of your sanity, these demons of self-hate, rage, fear, just keep knocking; keep on saying, let us out. We want out of here. We have to go. We want to go. We want to go and curse out your mother. She did not give me a dollar for a drink. We want to go out and kick some ass. Your best friend was kissing your girlfriend. I want to go kick his ass.

We want to get out. We want to go drink some liquor or take some hard drugs. We want to get out. You shall have no relief. The daylight will be a long time coming if you do not let us out. Get us out of here!

Self-Love or Self-Destruction

The Black Family

When denial and blame turn to sorrow and shame, then your body (neck-belly-chest) takes the pain.

At the risk of being repetitious, I repeat, in order for us to be whole again.

We must first admit that we Blacks in the western world are living emotionally handicapped. Picture a race horse with a 200 lb. jockey on its back, and all the other horses, including himself, keep asking how come he can't keep up with the race.

We should be so lucky as to just have a physical handicap. It's easy to see and remove a physical handicap. An emotional handicap is not easy to see and it's even more difficult to remove.

For us to be whole again, we must first admit that we were being sadistically robbed of our humanity, of our self-love that God gave us. What we have been taught now is how to hate, how to self-destruct. Like those little toy trucks that kids play with. Just wind him, turn him loose, and he'll run right into a pole.

Program to Self-destruct. Look at it this way. With a lack of self-love and self-esteem it's easy to abuse your body because in reality you are abusing something that you do not love. It's also easy to abuse someone else's body because without love for one's own body, there can be no love for anybody.

I believe that we will be whole again, but it takes time. It takes a long time to unlearn. It takes a long time to try to forget and forgive our oppressor who is still living amongst us. It takes a long time to lament and comprehend how a people with the good Bible in one hand could have a whip and chain in the other hand. How they could read the Bible and still treat another human with such cruelty.

It takes a long time for us to resolve the conflicts within us.

Conflicts, ambivalent feelings of love and hate, love of self, love of the oppressor, hate of self, hate of the oppressor. It takes a long time to travel through the valleys of the shadow of death; the valleys of hate,

Self-Love or Self-Destruction

The Black Family

anger, fear, sorrow, and shame; the dark roads of envy, jealousy and insecurity. It takes a long time but time is on our side.

We will get whole again because as we travel this valley the chariots of hope will get us through. The horses of the human spirit and the spirit of God will get us there. And, even though we travel through these valleys with the curse of the whip and chains still on our minds today, we can get out.

One day we will see the light. We will reach the high mountain. We will stand on the peak of self-love where we will know the joy of love. The joy and ecstasy of love. Love of self, love and respect for our brothers and sisters. Love and respect for our aunts and uncles, fathers and mothers. Love, understanding, caring, fulfilling the needs of our children. Then we will be able, willing and ready to teach our babies how to love, how to grow up without the emotional handicap that we just got rid of after 400 long, long years of oppression. And when we are whole again, we will be ready, willing and able to teach our children how to get an education instead of how to get high. We will be ready to teach our children how to help an old lady across the street instead of taking her purse and knocking her off her feet. We will be able to spend quality time with our children, loving them, teaching them how to be happy. Teach them how to care; care for themselves, care for us; so that when we get old, they do not just put us away in a nursing home, put us out of the way to die. They will not abandon us like we abandoned them.

We will be able to look at our sexuality as male to female and enjoy it as the greatest gift God gave to man. Enjoy sex in a clean and wholesome way. Because when we are able to enjoy sex in an uninhibited, clean way, we will not have to seek the pleasure of sex in so many perverted ways. Pornography will disappear because we will not be able to sell it. Fathers will not have to violate and abuse their little girl child for sexual pleasure.

I want to say a lot more about this, but it will have to wait for another chapter and another place, another time.

The Black Family

How Can We Return to Self-Love Again?

The road American society is traveling along is disheartening. We are going in the wrong direction. Each day, we, as a society, are going farther away from the love of self, the love of our neighbor, the love of our community. Each day we are moving closer to selfishness, greed, and power. We do not understand that self-love opposes selfishness and greed. Our society fails to understand we cannot have both.

If we give up seeking for true love we automatically give up on happiness whether we are conscious of it or not.

The biggest tragedy of this is that Blacks become a bigger victim of every disease that hits our society because of our emotional handicap caused by slavery and continued oppression. So we in the Black community have a lot of soul searching to do to get self-redemption.

If anyone doubts me it is because they are looking but cannot see. Look at our kids. Look in the jails. Look on the streets in any Black neighborhood in New York City. You will see people who have lost their identity, who have lost their love. You'll see people who are financially poor but even worse, who are poor in spirit and hope. We see contamination of the mind. We see children who gave up on life, who just stopped trying. Giving up leads to drug abuse, jail, violence, and alcoholism.

Ways to be Whole Again

First, let's start with our children. They need it most. We can teach them to love as opposed to hate and violence.

The only place a child can effectively learn is in his own home. He learns from his parents. As a rule, happy and loving parents will grow happy and loving children.

To teach an infant how to love, we must first love him. Black women who bring babies into this world must understand what motherhood is all about. True motherhood is putting the needs of the infant first. It involves a lot of caring, a lot of hugging, a lot of body contact, a lot of soft and

The Black Family

tender loving touches. This is especially important during the first few years after birth.

An angry and tired mother will feel the urge to act out on the child, contaminating the child with anger and self-hate. Black mothers should become conscious of this and guard against it.

We, as Black people, start realizing that a mother's love is the greatest gift that God gives to a child. With a mother's love, an infant will grow up to be all he or she was meant to be. Without it he is really nothing but flesh and blood, without any soul, without any spirituality. Just an empty shell.

After mother's love comes father's love. The ideal mode is for the mother and father to be in love and to both love the child. What a blessing that can be. That's how God meant it to be.

I believe that God smiles every time he sees two adults in love, both giving their love to their offspring.

The good thing about human existence is that the mother has to be there when the child comes into this world. So, a mother's love can be readily available.

So let me say to Black mothers, do not be selfish. Love your babies so they will learn how to love. I say to Black mothers, let's break the chains of sorrow and anger. Try as best you can. I know it's not always going to be easy, because you were not given love as a child and most of the time are still yearning for love and for some man to love. But the baby is innocent. He is not to blame. He needs love, just a little love. And, if you can do that, I can promise you that child will grow up to give that love back to you. You will not have to be afraid of him when he is 16 or 20 years old. He will be ready to be a man with love to give to his children. He will be able to love and respect his community and love his mother. I say love not pity. Love and discipline.

The Black Family

Love in the Family

The child also needs the love of a family. Brothers, sisters, grandmothers, grandfathers, aunts and uncles, to make up a family unit.

We well understand the difficulty of getting some Black fathers to live up to fatherhood. Too often we see Black babies without a father around. What a pity for the child. I hope soon, very soon, that will change.

This is why I cannot see how we can still blame the white man for our dilemma. Would we want the white man to come around and play father to our kids like they did during slavery? That's part of what got us into this dilemma we are in today.

So, fatherhood seems to be the biggest obstacle we must face before we can be whole again.

But what about unclehood? What about grandfatherhood? What about bigger brothers, aunts, and sisters? If every relative of a child would or could give a little love and attention to that infant child, what a blessing that would be! Then we would be on the road back to the good old days; back to solid and strong families like we had back on the West Coast of Africa hundreds and hundreds of years go.

Let me close by saying that rebuilding a strong and loving family system is the only way we can really hope to be ourselves again. Strong, loving families grow happy people, people who are free from the demons of anger, hate and fear. People with self-love. People who know how to love and be loved which is the greatest gift any human can have.

The goal of better family unity and harmony is not an easy one to achieve, because in American society as a whole, this is less important to us than, say, 20 years ago. Now, individual rights are what we are after. Family rights are hardly ever mentioned. Yet as I look around our society, the families of whites are in a lot better shape than Blacks.

If one takes a good look at the Black family today, one will become sad and disappointed at what one sees. Nobody needs to read a book to know that Black men with healthy father images are rare. They are few and far between, as we might say.

Self-Love or Self-Destruction

The Black Family

What can we do to have more fathers in our community? Where, how, and when must we plant the seeds? Where do we get the fertile land, the rain and sunshine, so we can reap the harvest of good fatherhood? Because what we are doing today is not working. The crop we are getting is far less than we should settle for. What we are doing as planters of humans is guilty of gross neglect towards our crops. If this was a court of law we would have to pay heavy damages or be sent to jail.

But, the price we are paying is no less than a jail sentence, because when the kids become adults, instead of becoming good fathers they go to jail.

The first lesson the male learns about fatherhood is as a child. There should be some male image for him to follow so that as a child he can see how a man should and does act. The paternal father should be the one but if he is not around, almost any male can provide a substitute.

He can take the little boy out, sit and talk with him, lift him up and hug him, tie his shoe laces, teach him to talk, help him to learn how to walk. That's loving him. That's teaching him how to love.

The girl baby also needs a father image. This, in a different way from the boy. She can have her first love affair with a man, a man that can love her without the little girl having to give up anything. She will just love a man and the man will love her back without any sexual implications. She can love a man before her sexuality is developed. And, most important of all in this union between father (or man) and daughter, the adult must not, **cannot**, put his adult sexuality on this innocent little girl.

The growth development of the child that takes place between the child and the adult of the opposite sex is a very delicate process. A freaky or perverted adult can surely contaminate the child. If this development does not occur the right way, the boy will grow up having difficulty dealing with women, and the girl will have difficulty dealing with men. There is not enough space in this article to do the subject any justice.

I believe a child without a father can grow up emotionally healthy. Especially if the other male members of his or her family can chip in and

Self-Love or Self-Destruction

The Black Family

give the child some love and attention, because a loving mother is the single most important need for that child.

The reason I am writing so much about this and even repeating myself many times, is that we can do it. We have the ability as Black people, the tools and the skills, to give some more love and attention to our children. The price we are paying now for failing to do it is too heavy.

I have seen mothers with daughters, say 12 or 14 years old, who spend no time with the child. The mother is too busy doing everything else. If the child doesn't get attention in a positive way, he or she will try to get it in a negative way by being rude and misbehaving.

The Black Family

Prayer For a Black Hero

Dear Lord, please send us a black hero
One who is worthy of thy praise.

Inspire him to love his fellowman
Give him kind and humble ways.

Someone to teach the children how to love and obey.
They have labeled us the black sheep
And it seems we have gone astray.

Our hopes, our joys, our priorities are all covered in a moral decay.

Oh Lord, please give us an answer
Tell us how and why we've failed.
Each time we think we have a hero
They wind up in the jail.

I know there are few among us,
Good Black men and women who can
Lead us to the Promise Land.
But they need your inspiration
Please touch them with your hand.

We as a people are captured in this foreign land.
Please send us a Moses or a Joshua.
Please, please, I know you can.

And as we pray, dear Father,
Bless us black sheep one and all.
Teach us to love and respect
Each other 'cause that's part of our downfall.

Self-Love or Self-Destruction

The Black Family

Elijah Mohammed

Elijah came down from the mountain with the Holy Quran,
He said to the Black people, I have a teaching for you that can help you
To love and respect yourself if I could lead you all by the hand.

They said, the White man gave us the Holy Bible
And promised us all a Cadillac and a white girl if we followed his plan,
Okay, so why should we listen to you Mr. Elijah,
When you're just a Black man?

So Elijah took his Quran and went in search of the falling,
He went to the prisoners and drug addicts to see if they would hear his
    calling,
Since prisoners feel betrayed by the white man's plan.
They listened to Mr. Elijah and Muslims spread through the land.

For our dignity, for our self-esteem,
And any good feelings about us,
Leaving the White man's plan alone,
Is certainly a must.

Even if the white man has good intentions, his plan has caused us grief,
He needs a plan to save himself before he can give us relief.

Self-Love or Self-Destruction

The Black Family

A Letter to My Motherland

I was hunting, doing some running, I was happy,
I was free,
Then there came to scare me, a white man who captured me.

To teach me to be obedient, his whip put a scar upon my face;
To show how he could control me,
He put a chain around my waist.

He led me through the forest, right down to the coast,
There I saw a big ship waiting,
He threw me in like toast.

A long, long time is passing as I struggle for my pride,
My self-esteem, my joy,
In the hole with chains around me,
I know they all died.

So confused and hopeless,
I must think about my fate,
It seems to me this experience
Is teaching me how to hate.

Self-Love or Self-Destruction

The Black Family

Doomed, I gave up the struggle,
So I put myself in the white man's hand,
Thank God I was still alive when they led me
Out onto a foreign land.
I begged the Lord for mercy on my soul,
He made the white man so cold.

They sold me to the highest bidder,
He took me away grinning his teeth.
I said to myself, how come he's so happy?
Is he going to eat me like meat?

They took me in front of a great big house
And it all was so strange,
Then he said to his assistant man,
His name and nature we have to change.

Self-Love or Self-Destruction

The Black Family

So They Changed Me

So they changed me, so they changed me,
Even before I reached the Jamaica shore.
They put me to cut sugar cane,
And then they changed me some more.

For me to be the white man's mule, he had to change my nature,
So to him I gave respect and fear
And to myself I am a stranger.

He molded me into what he wanted me to be
And that is nothing like what I am,
Now I care only to please my master,
And for myself, I don't give a damn.

So I am living in a world outside myself
'Cause my true nature is changed.
Instead of loving me, I am weak and sorry,
And to my own self, I am strange.

The white man thinks he is so smart
Because he changed me and things are going his way.
The change was so good, so deep,
That I am at his mercy to this very day.

He spent so much time and energy to affect my change,
That he cannot see what it's doing to him,
He's created a monster, a Frankenstein,
Coming back to haunt his kin.

Self-Love or Self-Destruction

The Black Family

Our Nature in Common

All human nature is the same whether we are black, brown or white,
If you put a man's back against the wall,
His true nature is to fight.

We were born with the same nature, but something went wrong in the
    way we were raised,
We were taught to suppress our feelings,
That's what changed our nature in so many ways.

If we all had true self-expression,
Every human would be equal and the same,
But with our true self burned in childhood and forgotten,
We wind up with a guessing game.

If the child's true nature must be suppressed and forgotten,
Then the adult's human nature cannot be defined.
Ten million people with ten million different ways,
Some good, some bad, some have an indifferent mind.

Unable to express his true feelings of anger, joy, love, the sex drive,
Puts man in terrible shape.
In order to find the happiness of expression,
We have to seek perverted escape.

So we come into this world with a nature that is the same for every human,
But to raise a human child is most difficult and we pay the cost
'Cause by the time you reach adulthood, most of your true self is lost.

Self-Love or Self-Destruction

The Black Family

Unwanted Hate

What must I do with this anger and hate I have for the oppressor man?
It's beating, pounding, all inside me, like a drummer in a ban.'
If I should ever let it all out, I'd kill, kill, and go to jail,
I'd be so evil and violent, they would not give me bail.

So you see I'm in a dilemma, 'cause myself my need to control,
But this hate and anger is squeezing me,
There is a storm down in my soul.

If he had left me in my father's land, I'd be a free man today
But he captured me and enslaved me,
So anger and hate is the price I have to pay.

Inside me there's a storm, but outside I must act calm.
With this conflict I can see
I never will be free,
So please, good Lord, help me.

Self-Love or Self-Destruction

The Black Family

Thou Hath Enslaved My Soul

Oh thou great oppressor,
Thou hath enslaved my soul.

Thou hath set my body strong and free
But my spirit is still out in the cold.

Please, please set my soul free.
Let my soul drink from the cup of freedom
So my spirit and soul can join my body.

My soul, my hope, my self-esteem
Are still captured by your whip.
The chains upon my emotions are still laying on your slave ship.

Without my soul and body reunited,
I am just an empty shell.
How can I drink from the sweet cup of life
When you have put on me a spell?

I was happy when you set free my body
'Cause my soul I cannot see.
It took 400 years to realize
That inside I am still in misery.

Self-Love or Self-Destruction

The Black Family

Living Black in a White World

*B*eing Black in a world that's white,
You're always so ashamed you only want to come out at night.

The day at the parade, you feel like you bring the rain.
A day at the ball park, you feel like you are a PAIN.

You have to work each day on a job where you feel like you don't belong,
You're always feeling like the weak one
When you know you're big and strong.

You cannot go to a classy restaurant
Without feeling you're out of place.
You cannot even blend into a crowd
Because of the different color of your face.
Your kids go to school, they call them a nigger.
I feel like getting my gun, going back there and pulling the trigger.

Can I ever escape this prison with these bars?
Can I ever fly away to Venus, Jupiter or Mars?

There is no escape.
Only death can set me free.
And when I get to heaven,
I hope the good Lord will not reject me.

Self-Love or Self-Destruction

Black is Beautiful

I see so many of us Black people
Trying to change the way we look,
Straighten my hair, straighten my nose,
We are judging the cover of the book.

God made all men good looking and equal,
Trying to change it is a sin,
I didn't care about the character and dignity of this girl at the store
As long as she had light skin.

Even though I know Black is beautiful,
I still have a strong urge to change.
How can I ever win?
There are demons inside me telling me to be good, I must have white
    skin.

The Black Family

The Black Sees Himself

Of all the things I care about,
I care most about my soul.
I always pray for peace within myself,
I care not for people who are cold.

If my happiness means peace within
And how I see myself,
Then why the hell for 400 years is someone
Trying to make me into someone else?

Maybe the thought of a Black man being happy
Will scare him half to death.
He done lost the peace within himself
So he worried with deep regret.

If I can pick myself up with my own personality,
Teach my children to love and respect themselves,
Then I'll make my own destiny.

If the white man could just leave me be,
Stop telling me I am no good,
I could learn to have faith, hope and confidence in myself.
I could learn to be what I should.

Self-Love or Self-Destruction

Black Man Inside Himself

Traveled down inside myself
I saw an emptiness.
I did not see any color or shame
But I saw a moral abscess.

I had a conversation with my spirit and my soul.
We talked about comfort and joy and happiness
As we grow old.

They say, what's wrong out there?
How come you don't care about me?
You're just seeking after the fat of the land
Forgetting all about your spirituality.

Fat can give you a belly full.
Today you'll feel quite safe and sound,
But without the soul, the spirit in the play,
Your house is on sandy ground.

We talk about the white man
Holding up a package promising happiness and security.
They say stop being a fool for him
'Cause my only happiness is inside of me.

The Learning Defense

I see many, many Black people with what I call a learning defense.
The way they are an expert on everything
Is nothing short of nonsense.

If you put a book before them
They'll tell you they know what's inside.
They cannot admit that they do not know
Afraid it will hurt their pride.
They know everything about movies, politics, the law,
They will even play psychologist.
They always tell you what they can do, where they have been.
I've seen many a Black rocket scientist.

A man who's afraid to say I am wrong or I do not know
Is one with weak self-esteem.
His false pride and his boasting make him feel important,
Or so it does seem.

Anger—Love the Mule—the Slave

When God made all animals He gave them the ability to love and hate.
The ability to love and the ability to get angry you cannot separate.

With a whip upon the slave
He damaged our ability to express love, anger and joy.

Watch them breaking in a mule.
He is afraid to kick, he becomes the beast of burden.
In slavery they broke us in,
Domesticated everyone to obedience,
So a man felt like a little boy.

When you're broken in and domesticated
You cannot be sophisticated.
Your only desire is to obey.
You cannot express yourself.
You always feel like someone else.
It's like your feelings are made of clay.

Self-Love or Self-Destruction

Equality

As I look to the sky and see birds flying around
I often wonder if they feel superior to the chickens on the ground.
Does the white lion say to the black one, I am better than you?
Does the tall tree say to the shrubbery, I am going to take away your morning dew?

To watch a little river, how it flows gently into the big sea,
Oh, how great is Mother Nature, she gave the birds and the bees and the flowers equality.

What's wrong with us humans, I am trying to understand.
God made us equal, but each of us wants an upper hand.

The Black Family

The White Man

You're looking at me, white man,
Are you looking down on me?
You think when God made us all, he gave you superiority?

When you look at a Black man,
Tell me just what you see.
Can you see me as your brother with full equality?

Superiority is a demon that can only teach you to hate.
It does a lot for your ego, but oh how sad your fate.

If you can learn to love me, and see us each as one,
Your heart will be open,
And you'll be a better man.

Or you can stay upon your high horse and cherish your superiority.
I am sure it'll make you feel good for a while,
But only equality can set you free.

Self-Love or Self-Destruction

The Black Family

Black is Equal

*T*ell me, am I equal to every other man?
Is this a skin disease I've got?
I worked so hard to be a have,
But all the time feel like a have not.

Is the only thing that separates me, makes me different, the color of my skin?
Or has my blackness infected my blood, my heart, my liver, has it gone deep within?

How shallow minded are those men who judge me only on what they can see.
Give them an X-ray of my heart, my kidney, or what about my spirituality?
Tell me, Mr. White Man hard and cold,
What's the color of my soul?

Stop your superiority.
Stop looking down on me.

How come you cannot see
That the most important part of me
Is the same as everybody?

Self-Love or Self-Destruction

The Black Family

How It Feels To Be Black

When I came into this world, I knew something was wrong.
I was smart, loving and handsome but worried all along.

Why I kept having these feelings, I could never figure out.
I had all that should make me happy. What's holding me back?

It was the wisdom of my uncle that told me,
"Boy, it's just because I am Black."

Can I feel good and be Black at the same time or is being Black a crime?

No matter how hard I try to feel good, I wind up feeling low down and dirty from time to time.

Even with some education and plenty of money, I feel like I don't have a dime.

Since being Black is my fate, I can see no change, then I beg for the Judgement day.

And when I'm back in the new world, please, God, take this curse away.

You can give it to the White man. This time it's not my turn.

Let him feel how low down it feels to be Black.
He won't like it but he's gonna have to learn.

Let him walk a mile in my shoes, then tell me how it feels.

He'll be so sad and broken, he'll come to me crying, crying,
Black man, let's made a deal.

Self-Love or Self-Destruction

The Black Family

The Good, the Bad and the Me

*T*he good, the bad, and the me side of me.
Sometimes good, sometimes bad, and the little known side makes three.

When I went to school
They taught me how to be good,
To obey the Golden Rule.

When I want to have fun or when people mess with my space,
I want to fuss and fight and get drunk and break up the place.

Somewhere in the middle is the side that I rarely see.
I see the good, I see the bad, but where is the me side of me?

When they brought us out of the African land
They made sure the real me was lost.
They told me to be happy and act like I'm white,
And forget about my past.

I tried to do as they said
And forget about the real me,
But what I have in my dreams at night
Is a stranger I always see.

Self-Love or Self-Destruction

The Black Family

The stranger says, "I'm your pride, your self-esteem,
I am your integrity.
I am neither good or bad," he says,
"I am what you were meant to be."

I wake up full of hope 'cause the real me did appear.
I want to go back to dreaming again so
I can hug him and show him I care.

Whenever I am awake, the real me does not show.
The good side wants to keep up with the Jones
And the bad side wants to have fun and go, go, go.

Living Black in a white world the real me doesn't fit in.
Denial and suppression make me so confused, me, me, where have you been?

Self-Love or Self-Destruction

The Black Family

Black, Get Back

Black, Black, get back,
We are still at the back of the bus.
They said we could use the front seat
But that was only a promise, not a pledge
So now we must retreat.

We are back to the good old days
When Black kids did not need to go to school.
Welfare, drugs, violence, tell us what good for us it is
To use two sets of the golden rule.

Black, Black, get back
To when the Black man was shy and afraid.
Too much forward movement,
Before you know it he'll want to be mayor,
The grandmaster of the parade.

Get back to where you came from, picking cotton and shining shoes.
Get back to where your mothers and fathers
Gave the white man respect while singing the blues.

We let you sit in the front seat but now you want to own the bus,
We gave you a job in the office and now you want to be the boss,
And if you don't get it, you fuss.

So, Black, get back, get back.
We'll never again let you see the light.
You've been shining it all over the place.
So we can't sleep at night.

Self-Love or Self-Destruction

The Black Family

How the White Man Sees Me

I wonder how the white man sees me.
I think he still sees me as a fool.
As long as I am willing and able,
I'm okay, that's cool.

If I just look at him and smile
And let him treat me like a child,
As long as I stay in my place
He'll let me dance if I believe that white is the better race.

But when my feelings start to bubble,
Boy I am in trouble
If I ever want to feel good
And live in a better neighborhood.
If I try to work hard and fas' so I can be the boss,
Don't ever express my feelings true
And try to tell him what to do.

He'll praise me for sweeping the floor
But to mingle at the party he'll close the door.
He'll tell me I am a hard working man
As long as he drinks from the golden cup
And I from a tin can.

The white man has a conscience, you see,
But it'll last only as long as I leave him be.
He must sit on top of the world
While I pull his wagon like a little sissy Black girl.

Self-Love or Self-Destruction

The Black Family

Black in the Mirror

I am looking in the mirror,
I see a man they call Black,
My skin is brown, my beard is white,
My mind and intellect has no color,
That's a fact.

If Black is the reason why I feel like an inferior man,
Do white people feel inferior when they stay in the sun and get a tan?

My eyes and senses are telling me my color does not say who I am,
But my mind from childhood was programmed to believe
I am only equal to a goat, the ram.

I look upon my children and sometimes wish that they were white,
'Cause every time they walk up to a mirror
They feel like turning off the light.

So mirror, mirror on the wall
Who is the most superior of us all?
What if I paint white my hands and face?
Can you put me in the white man's place?

Self-Love or Self-Destruction

The Black Family

Friendship from a Black Perspective

Friendship is giving, friendship is forgiving.
Selfish people do not make good friends.
Egotistic people do not make good friends.
People who see themselves as better than others do not make good friends.
People who feel the world owes them something do not make good friends.
People with a lot of suppressed anger do not make good friends.

I call these traits the enemy of friendship: selfishness, egotism, suppressed anger.

The main reason why these enemies are so strong and common is that most people who possess these traits will strongly deny having them and, worse, these people will be the first to accuse others of possessing these demons.

I have learned so much about these people, I can spot them right away.

I used to work with some fellows who were always calling everybody they met stupid, selfish and dumb, not realizing that their observations were just a reflection of themselves.

A selfish man becomes very disturbed when he sees selfishness in another man. He cannot stand it. He is troubled and confused by it, while a not-so-selfish man can be indifferent.

What makes a good friend?

Well, I am no expert at the subject but what I have read, plus 50 years of life experience have taught me a lot.

I believe a good friend must first be a person who can accept that there is nothing for nothing in this world. To have a friend, he must be a friend. To some people friendship means only what can you do for me.

Self-Love or Self-Destruction

The Black Family

As a child that kind of thinking is OK, but then again, some adults always think like children.

The best way to do this is if you meet a person that you like, the first question to ask yourself is, "What can I do for this person?" I would like to be his or her friend. What can I do to show my friendship?

Look how beautiful it would be if both parties thought along those lines. Then the stage is set for a long friendship.

This is easier said than done—especially among Blacks. Most of the time, even if one person is thinking what can I give, the other is thinking what can I get, which leaves room for a one-sided friendship.

There are a lot of so-called friendships that are one-sided. They do not last long. They may last for a while if the giving person is a weak person with low self-esteem, who does not think of themselves as worthy of an equal relationship. But eventually, the weak person will feel used and abused they will have no choice but to end the relationship. The one will feel used, and hopefully, the other will feel guilty for expecting and participating in a one-sided relationship.

The Personality for Friendship

Oftentimes we meet people who struggle very hard to be a friend but they mess up again and again. The lucky ones are those of these people who can be humble, let themselves come down to the reality of these personalities, and start over again. Some people just do not have the personality for friendship.

Some people are so empty inside that they spend most of their time trying to fill that emptiness. No time to think about anybody else, about wife, children or friends. Most of these people wind up sad and lonely, or spend all their time at the office or involved in some other hyped up activity, or go from relationship to relationship.

Then there are people who are very loving and giving but still struggle to hold a long-term friendship. That's because they can get hurt so easily. Thin skin, so to speak. These people may have a touch of paranoia. They

Self-Love or Self-Destruction

The Black Family

find it hard to trust anyone. They always believe somebody is trying to hurt them. If you look into this person's past you see that they have been hurt before, most times by their parents. They want to trust, they want to love and be loved. They want it desperately, but like the song says, "Love don't come easy for them."

People with a lot of mistrust can get rid of it only by a conscious effort to resolve the hurt inside them. They can learn to trust again.

Black Men

Black men, in general, have a weak system of trust caused mainly by the loss of our manhood caused by over 400 years of oppression. We often find it hard to give love and respect to even our wives and children, and it also affects our personality when we try to build friendships.

I for one, for most of my life, could only experience one really passionate feeling towards a woman—a feeling for sex. If I could not sex her up, then I had no use for her. I'd be wasting my time with her.

A man that can only look at a woman for sex, or a woman who can only look at a man for sex, is a sad person who is isolating themselves from half of the human race. That's cheating on one's self.

Blacks, in general, need a lot of lessons on how to build friendships with people of the opposite sex. Very few of us know how to do that.

We, Blacks, actually look down on our women. Screw them and leave them. Even some of us Blacks, who claim to be so nice to women, are just being good in order to control, not really for friendship.

Boy meets girl. But feels he has to give girl material things to get what he wants. He has to buy her love. Or in one sense, he is saying to himself, I am not really good enough for this girl to love me but I know how to get her love. Buy her a TV, a fur coat, gold chains, and make her love me. A man with that kind of thinking usually winds up feeling sorry for himself.

The woman who falls for material things as a substitute for love is in the same sad shape as the man.

The Black Family

When it comes to kindness, with emotionally sound people, kind words, tender touching, a genuine desire to know how the other person feels, a lot of listening and talking, all work much better than just giving things.

Friendship is a bridge that brings two people together. It brings two hearts, two bodies, and two souls together. The two people must meet in the middle of that bridge together and bring heart, body and soul with them. Some burn it before crossing.

If one person brings just the body and not his heart, if one person just stays on his side of the bridge saying to the other person, you come and get me, come and rescue me, I am afraid to cross that bridge, it won't work. Heart, body and soul must meet half way to have a sound and lasting friendship.

The Black Family

I Dump on my Kids

If you dump on me, then I go dump on my kids.
That's not the way it's supposed to be,
But that's the terrible way it is.

We as Black people were oppressed,
And it left us with heavy sorrow,
It left us in a mess.

Oppression made me feel useless,
I lost my self-respect.
Please give me back my dignity
That's why I am so upset.

If I am always upset and angry
And you are much bigger than my size,
The innocent and helpless, my kids,
Are the ones who get victimized.

Give me back my self-respect so I can learn to live
Give me back my self-respect so to my kids
I'll have it to give.

Self-Love or Self-Destruction

The Black Family

The Black Family in America

I have a deep urge to write about the Black family in America. I believe the issue has been neglected for far too long, so I'd like to do my little part to bring this issue up to the front burner of our consciousness in the Black community.

We can wait around for the white community to bring this issue to the front. But we can be sure that if and when they do, it'll only be to the point where it serves their own cause.

The demons that plague Black communities can also be found in white communities, but we have them wider, deeper and far more abundantly. We have worse, much worse, than them.

The worst part of what's wrong with Blacks in America today is the decaying disintegration, the breaking up of the Black family structure.

It seems to me that all living things on the earth like to bunch up together. They like to form a community of birds, trees, flowers and animals, and it seems to me that each of these communities has harmony within them except one—humans. I believe God gave humans too much power, so we use it and abuse it.

In the human community the family structure is most important. A lonely human is a sad human. A human with people around him but who still feels alone, who feels that nobody loves or cares for him, is a very, very sad human. In his mind, he does not have a community.

When the oppressor brought us here as slaves that's exactly what he did to us. He broke up the family, took away our community, and left us till this very day, feeling sad and lonely, shameful and very angry.

Black brothers and sisters, let's not be so naive or foolish as to believe the white man is going to fix the system he broke and cares nothing about. We have to fix it ourselves or it won't get fixed. The emotional enslavement

The Black Family

of Blacks will last for another 400 years or more if we can't fix it. So what to do? Where must we start?

We have to be builders, each and every one of us. Our job right now in 1993 is to rebuild the Black family. We have to build it from the ground up, start from the foundation so we can have a strong house and home.

As I write these words, the words of this song come to mind, "A house is not always a home." We in America, we build a lot of great big houses, but very few homes. So the solution for Blacks today is to start building strong solid homes. The family, the home, is the core, the center of any community

A House is Not a Home

We do a good job at building houses. Now we need to start building solid, strong homes.

To build a loving home and family we must start with two people—man and woman who decide to start a relationship.

To build a good relationship today is not as easy as it seems. Building relationships is not a treasure in our society today. Building fame and fortune are.

There are many enemies of a good relationship today. I believe the most prevailing ones are selfishness and mistrust. I believe the main ingredients in the recipe for good relationships are:
- Trust
- Respect
- Understanding
- Love
- Child

The Black Family

Let's consider them one by one.

Trust

Very few people are ready to say to another, I do not trust you. The mistrust is hidden and denied. Most times, even the owner of that mistrust is not in touch with it.

People who have been hurt before, especially as children, and sometimes as adults, have a very deep-seated mistrust at the core of their personality. They can learn to trust again but it is a very difficult task ahead.

Understanding

If we can give a little trust then we can start the process of trying to understand the person I am trying to fall in love with. Through understanding is where, I believe, some of the selfishness issues can be resolved.

We can understand that as an adult it is unrealistic to expect to find someone to take care of you, to find love on a one way street. We can understand that two people have two sets of needs. Give and take are the key words here. It takes a lot of talking. Talking, not just about the weather, but about each other's wants and needs, each other's likes and dislikes. The way things are going today, most of us feel that our need is most important. It's OK to say that, but it's not a good ingredient for a relationship recipe. Trust and understanding and then...

Respect

Respect can work wonders for a relationship. If you can define and respect each other's rights, half the battle is won. When love is strong and all is well, respect is easy. But when there are a lot of problems in the relationship and it seems one person is taking too much from the other, respect can add a lot of tolerance to one's personality.

Self-Love or Self-Destruction

The Black Family

Sometimes we believe the other party is doing wrong but with respect and understanding the imperfection of all humans can be greatly tolerated.

Love

Love is the most important ingredient in the recipe for a good relationship.

Love is a mystery, love is magic, love is mighty peculiar. You cannot hurry love, you cannot push or shove love. You plant the seed and if you're lucky, it grows. Just like the flowers grow through rain, love can grow through pain. But it ain't easy because most of us don't have the courage to stand a little pain. So there's not enough time for love to grow.

I believe a relationship can be good if the two people work at it. With trust, understanding and respect, the land is fertile for love to grow. So we can build a beautiful house and home, which is the start of a solid Black family.

The Child

When two people find harmony, unite and share their lives together, share sex with love, then there is no more appropriate time to have children. Having a child is the second most important thing a human can do. The first is to protect his own life and to keep the human race going by having children.

It's been observed that the sex drive and desire to eat are the two strongest instincts of animals. Eating preserves the life of the self and sex preserves the continuation of the race. That's why when we try to go after wealth and power at the expense of the self we are sadly disappointed.

We often see commercials that say buying a house is the most important decision you can make. I say bull! It's the idea of putting a house as more important than a child that got us into the dilemma we are in today.

The woman and the man should sit and talk much about having children. Is the man ready for the responsibility of being a father or does

The Black Family

he just want to have fun screwing? Is the little girl ready for this responsibility or is she just spiting her parents, or does she think having a child will make her feel like she is somebody?

Having a child for the wrong reason will place the burden of resentment on the child.

I have a friend whose behavior always puzzled me. He was always angry, always blaming people around him for his anger and misfortune. On the other hand, he was a very good person. So why is this good person always in trouble? I found out.

I asked his mother one day, how come you and your son don't get along? I was shocked at her reply.

His mother started talking about how bad and evil his father was. But my friend was always telling me about the sadistic treatment he got from his mother. I concluded that his anger and the trouble he had just to make it in life, was a rotten father and a revengeful mother who took her revenge out on her child, an easy target.

I talk about my friend's dilemma, but mine was under the authority of an angry mother who had no self-love, and a chronically indifferent father. My mother was one of the best people I knew, and also one of the angriest. Don't ask me how one person could possess so much good and evil at the same time. It is confusing to say the least. But she had a whole lot of good in her.

At Christmas she gave the baker money to bake buns and had me distribute them to all the very poor people in the village. But she constantly beat me, tied me up, and beat me some more. I was the victim of a very, very angry mother. She was possessed by a demon handed down from her own parents who abandoned her.

The reader might say I am a good parent because I do not beat my child. I say it isn't necessarily so. There is also a demon called neglect. Neglect can give rise to the same symptoms in a child as beating him or her. Neglect leaves the child empty, alone, full of deep fears, feelings of abandonment, and also a lot of anger and mistrust.

Self-Love or Self-Destruction

The Black Family

Parents, do not try to seduce or smother or overly control your child. They'll grow up angry with you because you did not give them a chance to express themselves. Self-expression is the key to happiness.

All these demons described above can severely hinder a child's self-expression, leaving him angry and dissatisfied about himself and about his true identity.

Love, Discipline and the Child

I feel a need to explain about love, discipline, pity and raising a child.
Pitying a child, giving him or her all the material things you can afford
Is not the same as love (I repeat, it's not the same as loving the child)

Pitying and refusing to discipline the child
Is not the same as loving the child.
Discipline is very important in any human life.
We learn to respect other's rights,
We learn to stay away from things that're harmful to our well being.
Discipline us, teach us how to handle money—use some and save some.

Fatherhood

In our society today when we do not put a lot of honor and value on fatherhood we suffer for it. So, please mother, ask an uncle, brother or grandfather to help with the raising of the child. Without a father he can still grow up a bit healthy.

I believe one of the most delicate things to do is to bring up a child who is emotionally healthy. This process takes at least 10 long years. A donkey or a calf can get up and walk a little by itself after birth. So, please, Black parents, don't treat your newborn like a donkey or calf. The child needs care, love, and some discipline. Too much, too little, too late, and the child loses his self-expression and becomes resentful and angry, most of the time without even knowing it. He thinks this is a normal way of life for him. He can never figure out why he doesn't trust anyone, why he always feels the rest of the world is looking down on him or her.

Give a child attention in a positive way or he/she will soon learn to get attention in a negative self-destructive way, even when he/she grows older.

So, I have given the recipe for building a good house, a home, a family. Stir well and let cook for 10 years so we Black Americans can be whole again. So we can recapture our self-love, our self-respect, our self-esteem, our self-redemption and glory, hallelujah, our self-determination.

The Black Family

Don't Touch my Glass

Are you sure all the nice gifts you gave me are for love and not control?
Do you want my heart, my body? How can any love be so cold?
I am trying my best to love you.
I am doing the best I can.
But each time your heart is burned you start to raise your hand.
Did your mother and father love you?
Can you love me right?
Why must we live in misery?
Why must we fuss and fight?
When you get distressed and angry and it seems this day will not pass,
Hit the pillow, hit the couch, but PLEASE do not touch my glass!

Self-Love or Self-Destruction

The Black Family

Suppress the Hurt, Embrace the Comfort

As a little child I lost my reason to smile.
It hurts always to feel alone,
Even though I had the comfort of food and a home.
When I was 17 I had an insecure dream,
I learned to suppress the hurt and to embrace the comfort.

At a teenage party one night,
I had a girl that was just right.
Her embrace was soft and bold
It thrilled me to my soul.

I had so much comfort and joy,
Till I saw her in the arms of another boy.

I tried to suppress the hurt and embrace the comfort,
But the hurt keeps bubbling to the top
Each time the comfort level drop.

Each time some comfort fall,
The hurt makes me feel small.
Somebody please tell me how to feel,
I need the comfort of more than a good meal.

Self-Love or Self-Destruction

The Black Family

To comfort me each day,
I need to hear somebody say
"Thanks Ash, you're O.K."
But the hurt began to rise
Each time I close my eyes.
It comes up so strong,
Always makes me feel wrong.
As the comfort level fall,
Makes me feel small.
Somebody throw a kiss my way,
Help me make it today.

Self-Love or Self-Destruction

The Black Family

Can't Find a Home

Woke up this morning, got loving you on my mind.
Tried to get you on the telephone,
All the pay phones were off the line.

Spent most of the night begging something to eat,
Went down to the railroad station to try to find somewhere to sleep.

I am writing this letter across an old newspaper line,
I'll put it in your mailbox,
I hope you'll wake up on time.

Since you talked to me at the station,
You alone give me a reason to live.
If you're not ashamed to see me again,
Please bring something, anything you have to give.

I am not ashamed to tell you I have nothing to wear,
I need a shave and a shower,
And some tender loving care.

Many, many years for me on the couch,
Taught me to see people's sorrow.
I looked upon your face and saw some sadness and pain,
Beyond your beautiful smile, I see some sadness again.
I need not tell you my story
You know the shape I am in,
If we can unite our sorrows,
With the help of God we can win.

Self-Love or Self-Destruction

The Black Family

Sad My Dad

I am feeling lonely, I am feeling sad.
Can't seem to sort out my feelings about my Dad.

Hard working man, works like an ox every day.
Farming, butchering, from sun up to sun down,
Carrying big bags on his back.
This man had no time to play.

I am confused, I am perplexed.
As a father to a son, there was absolutely no communication.
He fed me, he clothed me,
Believe me he was good.
So how come food and clothes don't make me feel
Like a good boy should?

There is a burning feeling deep down inside of me
That he didn't understand how to love,
So he just lived up to his responsibility.
He used to sing as he worked,
A lonely man was he.
Pity he didn't know I was also lonely,
Or we could have kept each other company.

Oh, daddy, daddy, daddy, forgive my deep suppressed rage.
'Cause the first drop of tear I shed for you
Will dry up on this page.

Self-Love or Self-Destruction

The Black Family

The Barber's Chair

I sat in the barber's chair, a cool young man cutting my hair.
Clip, clip, clip with his scissors, brush and cutter.
Looking at him I think,
He is a street kid,
Someone, it seems, to have come from the gutter.

He was born in the city,
I grew up on the farm.
How much my thinking has changed.
I used to envy city boys,
They had all the bright lights, ice cream and toys.

But now I am older I found out
Climbing trees, milking goats, cutting bananas and eating them on the
    spot.
I had more good things that the city boy hasn't got.

I said to him, you know young man,
It's good you're making an honest living
Working as hard as you can,
You must have a hard time dealing with the social pressure,
'Cause today in 1992, working for an honest living,
Young people do not treasure.

Self-Love or Self-Destruction

The Black Family

Footsteps of Mama

I hear footsteps, a humming,
Are they coming to my crib?
Is that you coming mama,
Coming to teach me how to live?

My father-uncle, brothers and sisters,
I hear their footsteps everywhere.
If I stop crying mama,
Will you show me that you care?

The light of day is fading,
With the setting sun from above.
Please gather around my family,
Let's pray for the angel of love.

And mama, I often wonder,
Do you have a man who is kind?
Or does he try to fool you with silver and gold,
Does he have an angry mind?

Because if there is love between you two,
If there is love in my family, how lucky I will be.

Because you all could come over to my crib,
And love, love me.

Self-Love or Self-Destruction

The Black Family

Let me Drink

Give me lots of whiskey, let me drink more wine,
Give me a shot of vodka, it will suit me just fine.
Any kind of liquor will wash away this heartache of mine.

As long as I am drinking I can just stare at stars,
Can look up to a flying saucer and take off to Jupiter or Mars.

Give me more whiskey, it'll loosen up my face,
It will liquidate my troubles, and that will give me some space.
When I am drinking, keep on drinking, I don't feel the pain.
I can feel the sunshine while walking in the rain.

I can feel safe and easy when folks try to put me down,
Drinking gives me company when there's no one else around.

Give me whiskey, give me some wine,
A shot of vodka will do just fine.
Let me loosen up my face,
Let me liquidate my troubles and give my mind some space.

Self-Love or Self-Destruction

Positive Thinking

A thought expressed can bring you happiness,
A thought can make you blue.
You don't always have to do, do, do,
What you think is you.

When you are sailing, sailing in your boat,
Positive thinking, your thinking, makes it float.

Negative thinking, if negative you think,
Negative day dreaming will make your boat sink.

In my imagination I can see frustration,
Or I can be dining with a king,
I can be working at a gas station,
Pumping excitation,
Or complaining how come I never win.

If beauty's in the eye of the beholder,
Then what I think is what I see.
If my thinking gets too foggy,
Then lost, lost in the dark clouds I'll be.

The Black Family

Empty Bottle, Empty Room

Wake up sleepy, looking at the bottle on the floor,
Try to squeeze a drop from it but it's empty
That's it, ain't no more.

I am tired and angry,
An empty bottle and an empty room,
My life is empty,
I am going down to doom.

It's five o'clock in the morning,
At least the clock is working still,
I should go out and call my wife
But she's mad and I don't have the will.

Maybe I could find another woman,
One who likes a man who can drink,
One who won't be bothered
When I throw up in the sink.

This bottle is so good to me,
When it's full it keeps me company,
But when I awake and it's empty,
It fills my life with misery.

Empty bottle, empty room,
I cannot make it this way.
Give me a full bottle and a woman who can stand me
And I'll be happy every day.

Self-Love or Self-Destruction

The Black Family

Confession of a Junkie

Welcome my friend, Welcome.
You I love, worship, and adore.
But each time you promise me happiness, you don't deliver, you just promise me more.
You promise to lift my misery to lift me way up to the sky.
I cannot help but believing in you, it feels so good when you make me high.

A promise is a promise, Dear friend,
Can you deliver anyway?
My heart is heavy, my body is weak, when will I see the light of day.

All my friends and family are gone. I am a lonely man.
I am looking to you for comfort but I am not sure that you can.

Why can't I seem to shake you, you low down dirty outcast?
I need some strength and courage to kick this habit in the ASS.

Where I am going now my friend, you cannot come with me this time.
You promise comfort but deliver misery, this is the end of the line.

I was the biggest fool to believe you in the first place,
The only reason I let you in was because I fell from grace.

Please leave me alone 'cause now I can see, with friends like you who needs an enemy.

Self-Love or Self-Destruction

The Black Family

The Last Day of My Life

I am flying high, high on clouds of sorrow,
This chemical experience seals the fate of all my tomorrow.

I must get rid of you,
If I have to beg, steal or borrow.

Yesterday was the last day of my life.
Today I am left with just sorrow, pain and strife.

Yesterday into the bathroom I wept,
Opened the medicine cabinet trying not to get myself upset.

Stood there for a long while,
Staring at the pill,
Seems very tempting but
It goes against my will.

There's the razor blade in the corner,
But I don't really need a shave.
Turn and walk away my son,
Not your body but your soul you have to save.

Yesterday was the last day of my life.
Today, I am numb,
More chemical, more chemical please,
Somebody please give me some.

Yesterday was the last day of my life,
Today is just a memory of tomorrow's
Sorrow, pain and strife.

Self-Love or Self-Destruction

Knowing that You Love Me

Knowing that you love me
Lights my dark despair.
Every hug you give me
Brings music to my ear.

Knowing that you love me
Sets my joy to dance,
I can feel self assurance
When I am waiting for your romance.

Knowing that you love me
Helps me break the ice.
I can face the long day's journey
And not be afraid to roll the dice.

The Black Family

A Duet for Happiness

You don't have to take me to Paris or Rome to make my happiness
   come through,
All I need is for you to love me and that's what I want you to do.
You don't have to give me a gold chain when I'm sad and blue,
All I need is for you to hug me,
Just hug me, and that's what I need you for you to do.

No fancy dress or car,
Material things that cannot love me won't go very far.
All I need from you is that you hug and kiss me
To make my joy come through.

Chorus: Together...

'Cause when we love each other for sure,
We need hugs and kisses no more,
Because love is the most important thing
For all the joy and happiness it will bring.

And when we're having conversation,
I don't need a lot of explanation.
If you're feeling sad and have a worried mind,
Tell me about it, I'll try to be kind.
Towards loving you I'll do the best I can do,
'Cause when we love and share each other,
All our happiness and joy come through.

Self-Love or Self-Destruction

The Black Family

MLK Jr., Compassion and Wisdom

A man of sorrow, expressing his grief,
Of wisdom and compassion, his feelings were relieved.

A man who can walk with a beggar and a king one on each side,
He can make the king humble,
And give the beggar back his pride.

He wakes up in the mornings, and he is self possessed,
Can give vent to his feelings,
A man who is self expressed.

He's aware of all human conditions,
He gives only to give,
He has many blessings,
'Cause he lives to make others live.

A man with the ability to love in the face of injustice,
To ask for understanding and forgiveness
For those who called him a Communist.

Some say a wholesome man there could never be,
I say a wholesome and compassionate man was he.

Some say compassionate men are long gone,
I say Martin Luther King Jr. was one.

Self-Love or Self-Destruction

The Black Family

Lord, Forgive our Unbelief

Dear Lord, please forgive my unbelief, forgive my untrusting soul.
I pray that you can understand, please bring me in, out of the cold.
I pray, I pray for trust and faith,
Touch my heart and remove my doubts,
Please don't let me wait.
Touch my heart so I can be
Full of hope and joy,
Remove my misery.
I keep on searching because you say, seek and you shall find.
To find a way to believe in you, to find a way to be humble and kind.

Lord I pray for all humanity
'Cause we took thy beautiful creation and gave back doubt to thee.
The mountain guides the river that flows into the sea,
So much a part of thy marvelous work
But like fools we fail to see.

Send thy angels down on this doubtful land to turn our thoughts above,
Teach us to remember thy greatfulness
And teach us how to love.

Fill our souls with joy and faithfulness,
Put them where our doubt has been,
Forgive us as we turn to earthly success
That causes this emptiness within.

Self-Love or Self-Destruction

Lord, My Spirit Looks up to Thee

O Lord, my spirit looks up to thee,
My soul cries out for thy company.
When earthly strife causes my soul grief,
I can look up to thee and feel relief.

When my everyday struggle seems all in vain,
I look into my tomorrow and it's dark again.
Then my spirit moves towards thy grace
And my soul is lifted to a heavenly place.

Touch me Lord and let me see,
'Cause without thee I've lost my spirituality.
Open my heart so I can be full of joy
With my trust in thee.

Lift my spirit, enchant my soul
Bless me Lord and make me whole.

Teach me more compassion to give,
Open my heart and help me live.

Thy praises more that I should sing,
To adore thee more than material thing.

My body is full with food and drinking
But my soul is empty and my spirit is sinking.

Fulfill me with thy grace abound,
And plant my feet on solid ground.

The Black Family

A Black Anthem

Onward, upward, and forward,
We're moving towards God's grace.
Onward, upward and we're saying,
"Human is our race."

We have prayed to the God above,
Teach us how to love.
He loves us, even the blackest face
'Cause he does not judge color and race.

Every one is born equal
And equal all must die,
Though it's impossible to be superior,
There are lots of fools who try.

From Mississippi to South Africa
The winds of change must rage,
The ink is black, the paper is white,
But it's an integrated page.

From slavery we are marching
To the day we shall be free,
We're not asking, we're taking
Our humble victory.

From Garvey to Mandella,
The ocean unites our grief,
Hopeful, strong and bold,
We're marching toward relief.

Self-Love or Self-Destruction

The Black Family

Give a Child Love

Give a baby the prettiest and the best things
And they will comfort his infancy in so many ways,
But give a baby love
And that love will comfort him for the rest of his days.

Give a child the opportunity to develop his talent to the peak
He can feel good about himself when he wins the big game or sings a
    number one hit song,
But give a child love and he'll feel good about himself alone in the desert,
In his weakest moments he'll feel strong.
Give the children love so they will give back to you,
Give the children love so they can always feel good about themselves
    and about the little things they do.

Give the children love, give them hope and joy abound,
Give the children love,
Plant their feet on solid ground.

Give a child love, he won't need greed and self-centeredness to make
    him feel secure,
Give a child love, he won't need to build an empire high up to the sky
To lift his feelings off the floor.

Give a child all the riches of the land
And it will last, he'll have plenty of adoration.
Give a child love, it will last and last and last to his third and fourth
    generation.

Self-Love or Self-Destruction

The Black Family

Welcome, welcome loving, black, beautiful baby boy. A world of joy is God's gift to you, and because you're so loving, and because you're so beautiful, our commitment to you is to see that promise come through.

Self-Love or Self-Destruction

The Black Family

Being Black and Male

If you are Black and male and reading this, welcome to this world where Black males have to live under the shadow of a sign that says you are not welcome. When you come into this world, nobody puts out a red carpet for you.

Your recent ancestors have been through an experience so brutal, so demeaning, it's a credit to their courage and strength that they lived through it.

That experience is slavery, an experience where one kind of man considers himself a man to the third or fourth power and all else are less than a whole unit, less than a man.

The man to the third or fourth power will bless his children with equal power and all other kids are cursed with feelings of never being able to feel like a full man. So the man who feels less than a man has to go to the man of four manpower and beg him for a little more power.

If you're a good boy and kiss my ass, I'll tell you that I love you. I'll let you sit with me, let you have one of our lesser females. That is, as long as you obey me and kiss my ass.

The thing that impressed me the most about Roots, the TV series, was at the beginning of the series, when we saw the father hold up the little boy baby and say, "Welcome to the world. Welcome, I'm going to teach you how to be a man. You're going to have a very healthy transition from baby to boy to manhood. We'll love you and teach you."

The father in Africa at that time was able to do that. He was able to welcome and love his baby son because there was no white man around. That father was free to love his child. Emotionally free.

If you are a Black male and you came into a world that was controlled or influenced by anyone but a Black man or a Black woman, then Black man you came into a world that will accept you only to the extent that he

The Black Family

can break you into obeying him and make you weak so he can capitalize on your weakness. He feels big because you're smaller. And he's not going to put out a welcome mat for you at any cost. You'll have to be broken in the hard way by force.

Now our ancestors in the white man's world were trained to stop loving themselves so they could obey the white man. The white man said to them, I'll feed you but only if you obey me. I'll feed your kids but only if they obey me.

So, the oppression of the Black man's spirit and his soul must continue for hundreds of years so that his body will survive. Our bodies survived slavery but our self love did not. Give up your true self, your spirit and your soul, for the greater good—the pain of our flesh and body.

To this very day in 1993, the Black man's mind is oppressed. His mind is enslaved so that his body might live. What a terrible choice. A choice no man should have to make.

Just like they do in slavery, a mother with two sons, she's given a choice, keep one because we are taking the other. She loves them equally. A hard choice.

So, the Black male came into a world where from the day he was born until the day he dies, he faces a daily struggle to fit into a world that cares very little about him. A struggle to feel equal. A struggle each and every day. When he looks in the mirror and sees somebody who looks different from the others, it's not hard to become convinced that he is different. And since I'M different and look different, am I different but better or different but less?

The Black male has a lot of disturbing questions. If I had a straight nose, straight hair, money to buy all the things that the white man has, will he accept me? Will I feel equal?

The answer to that question better be a bold yes. However, each layer of yes is laced with layers of uncertainty.

A big yes to the question of future acceptance is understandable because a no would mean loss of hope, a loss of expectation that keeps hope alive.

Self-Love or Self-Destruction

The Black Family

If you are a Black man reading this article try to be as objective as possible. This article is not a personal account of any one Black male, but of the male population in this white man's world.

O.K. Let's start from the beginning. A Black male is born into this uncaring world. At this time, he needs only two things to be happy and feel self-assured about himself (assuming he was born healthy)—food and tender loving care. Talking about uncertainty and anxiety, this little boy has a lot of it. The difficult task of the parents is to convince that baby boy he will be fed, he will be loved, and he will be welcome, arms are open for him. The first three years of this little boy's life are the most important ones of his whole life. Within these three years he will learn to feel either self-assured or full of self-doubt or be convinced that he is not important.

Let me pause here to say that adults often tell me how good or bad their parents treated them. The fact is, most adults do not remember being one or two or three. You can only tell the tree by the fruit it bears. If the adult is self-assured, the tree was raised in the right way, and vice-versa. That the parents did their best is not the issue. Most adults will accept their parents' treatment as good, and most parents will do their best for their children. So it's not easy to say your best was not good enough.

The fact is, the experience of slavery makes every human who lived through it very angry and an angry parent will raise an angry child. Furthermore, a parent who has to suppress that anger is likely to raise a child who suppresses a lot of anger too.

Back to the little boy. Before he gets to be three years old, he needs to have the comfort of a warm body, the warm breast of a woman. He can have his first love affair with a woman before his sexuality is developed. He needs not to be left alone for any length of time. He needs not to be punished for anything. He needs not to be punished for crying or for wetting his bed. He needs not to be punished for wanting more food or for wanting attention. All these things are the little boy's way of reaching out to his world for caring. If he is punished for it at this tender age he will begin to have doubts and will begin to withdraw. He will begin to

Self-Love or Self-Destruction

The Black Family

hold back. He will begin to have doubts about his acceptance in this world. He will start to become passive or angry and full of rage.

After about three years the little boy begins to feel his sexuality. He needs to see and react to a man around him to learn how to be a man. He also needs to feel some passion for the opposite sex. He still needs a tender body, a feminine body to hold and behold. Mother, sister or aunt can provide that. Father, uncle or brother can provide the male image for this little boy.

The little boy needs to have a relationship with a female that is deep and close so that when he grows up he doesn't just see women as sex objects or something just to have sex with. He can look at any woman on a brother/sister level too. Through being close with a woman during his childhood, the little boy will not see women as somebody on the other side of the track, someone he has to win, and someone who he has to cross a bridge to reach. He won't see women as someone he has to impress with a good image to win them over. He won't look at some woman as a prize or with the attitude, if she accepts me that means I'm good, but if she ignores me I'm no good.

At age 10 or 12 a boy will have these distorted feelings about the opposite sex which will live with him up until his twilight years.

A Self-assured Boy of 10 or 12

It is most difficult for a Black boy to feel self-assured. He feels that the white man does not accept him and is very uncertain about how he can get that acceptance he feels he truly needs.

Even more important than the acceptance of the white man, however, is the acceptance of his own family. Most of the time this little boy's father is physically and emotionally distant. Some sons will say well, my father was always in the house. But what about emotionally? Do you really know your father? Does he know what you feel? Does he know how you think? Does he know that you feel lonely all the time? Does your father spend time with you, talking to you and listening to you?

The Black Family

If the answer to the above questions is no, then the little boy is insecure. If there are other people like a kind and loving mother or other relatives, they can pull up the slack. Then the boy can be insecure but well adjusted emotionally. If the little boy feels that there is nobody around to really care about him (I don't mean just to feed and shelter him), if he feels unloved, then he doesn't just feel insecure. He is very angry. Angry at the world for neglecting him.

The experience of slavery taught Black men that loving their children was not the most important thing. If the boy is not sick or hungry, he's O.K. Some don't even care if the child is sick or hungry. So, because of the experience of slavery many, many years ago, most Black boys are insecure. Most Black boys have diminished self-love. Most Black boys see the world outside as unkind and unfriendly. A place where he's not equal to everyone.

Most Black boys see equality as something that he either has to work for very hard to get, or something that requires that he change something about himself in order to get it. If he's lucky enough to be strong and courageous, he can work hard to feel equal by climbing up the social ladder. These are the lucky ones. The lesser ones give up on equality. They say, what's the use and give up the struggle at 10 or 12 years of age. Then he turns to violence, alcohol or drugs, acting out his anger on a world that seems cruel to him. Crying for help. Crying for someone to care.

Sometimes his anger is turned on their own family. He has no love for anybody in this world. He's mean and angry.

Any human who feels unloved is mad, very mad. Love is a birthright and for those children did not get love, it's a violation of their birthright and they are mad for being robbed of it.

The experience of slavery robs everyone who was born under its influence—and the influence is still felt today, robbing them of their self-worth. The Black male gets the worst part of this disturbance. To be male means to be aggressive. It means to develop into manhood. The male instinct is a go-get-it one and if he cannot get it easily, then he has the

Self-Love or Self-Destruction

The Black Family

strength and courage to fight for it. The male boy's destiny is to grow up into manhood. His destiny is to grow up bold and brave, strong and aggressive, and to be happy.

It is difficult for any boy, Black, brown, white or yellow, to possess all or any of the above if he feels he came into a world that's looking at him as less than equal; looking at him as less than a man. Even when he becomes an adult he struggles to feel like a man. People treat him like an unimportant little boy.

If he feels that the way he looks and talks is not O.K. then he feels less than equal to the rest of his world and he has a lot of catching up to do to make himself equal.

The most important thing that can happen to a boy of 10 or 12 is to feel equal to everyone just by being alive and being in his world. He needs no car, no expensive clothes. He does not need to own or control some woman. He does not need to fight to show he's equal. I feel equal. I don't feel like anybody is better than I am, and I'm not better than anybody else is. I'm O.K.

The Male Instinct

The strongest instinct of all in humans is to seek love. The gratification of love is to gain good loving care as a child and self-love as an adult.

Now the male instinct is separated from the female instinct in that the male seeks to be developed into manhood. A fully matured male instinct is to continue seeking love and sex. Manhood means being aggressive, being bold and being brave. Aggression, boldness and bravery are necessary tools for maintaining survival. A man has to be bold and brave to protect his female, to protect his children, to protect himself, to find food while the mother is nursing the baby.

A man needs to be aggressive, a woman passive. That's why males with passive characters are called effeminate. Picture a healthy man who seeks the protection of a woman, as we sometimes see. For most of us Black men born in this part of the world, a world controlled by the white man, the development of our manhood instincts has been curtailed. It's always a struggle, a constant struggle to feel our strong manhood. We see our manhood mostly in terms of the way we behave rather than the way we feel. It's like saying, I'll show you I'm a man if you are in doubt. The fact is, though, that if I truly feel like a man I don't have to be quick to show it to anybody. My manhood is to be used to defend myself and my family, to protect myself and my family.

My manhood does not mean taking on some fool who's always looking for trouble. My manhood does not mean just screwing a lot of women and giving them babies. My manhood is fatherhood. It is feeding and protecting those babies. My manhood is not having to kiss the white man's ass so he'll let me sit beside him and smile at me. My manhood is to make me feel equal and strong no matter who's sitting beside me or even if I sit alone. I still feel equal and strong.

When I eat alone or eat with my family I feel strong. My manhood is to feel strong, to love and treat my brother with kindness, not to envy him and try to take what he has. With my manhood in hand I don't have to show off or lie to my friends about what school I've been to or how much money I have. Because, with my manhood in hand I always feel good about myself. No need for me to create a glorious image of myself to others to feel good. I can feel good about myself without having to worry about how they feel about me.

I'm only good if they see me as good. With my manhood in hand it's only how I see myself that matters. With my manhood in hand, I can look at a man with a Ph. D. and not have to feel that his Ph. D. makes him more than me. With my manhood in hand I can look at any other man, woman or child and feel convinced that their color does not make them more human than me. God makes us equal. The white man is not God even though he tries to play God by trying to make me less than equal. But if I have my manhood, if I have my self-assurance, he's bound to fail. As sure as there's a God above, he'll not succeed in making me less than equal to him. You see, if his manhood is what it's supposed to be, he

The Black Family

would have no need to see me as less. It's his own insecurity, his own uncertainty that gives him that need.

With my manhood in hand, I don't need to be violent. I don't need drugs or rum to make me feel strong. I don't need to take chemicals to suppress my bad feelings. With my manhood in hand all I need is love, good food, good sex, and a good family. Manhood is self-love, self-respect. Manhood is self-assurance. With my manhood in hand, I don't need a damn thing from the white man. If I work for him, he pays me well and I go home to my family.

Go home so I can love my children, love my wife, love my sisters, love my brothers. And if they love me back, that's my world. If we love and respect each other, that's my world.

I'm convinced the white man will never love me. Maybe he cannot because I look different from him and he has to share his glory with me. Maybe he cannot really like me. So the only happiness for me is to love myself and if and when I love myself then I don't really care if he loves me. If he does, it's good. But if he does not then I survive with or without his love and acceptance. Just pay me and leave me alone.

Leave me alone. I'll put a sign on my chest. Do not disturb because then my manhood will have to come to the front to defend myself, to defend my honor, defend my integrity.

Leave me alone so I can learn to love my kids, so my kids can learn to love me. Leave me alone so my kids' kids will know how to love their kids. Leave me alone so I can be myself, be what God intended me to be, to be a full man. Not half, not three quarters, but a full man. Leave me alone, because I'm working towards my own self-love, something you cannot give to me.

You need more self-love too, Mr. White Man. I'm working towards strengthening my own manhood, something you cannot do for me.

All the glorious material things that you adore and tell me to adore only cause me greed. Greed cannot make me happy, so what you have to offer me cannot make me happy. I need love. You, Mr. White Man, need

Self-Love or Self-Destruction

The Black Family

love. Everybody needs love. And, you will not or cannot give me love. So give me back the key to my happiness.

I hate having to beg you or any other man to open the door of happiness for me. I must have the key because with you having the key I have to beg and obey you to feel happy. I have to give up too much for your promise of happiness. When you shut the door I feel useless and afraid. How can I feel like a man if I feel useless and afraid?

I'm going to hold the key to my happiness so I can give it to my kids so they don't have to feel useless and afraid. They can feel strong and proud. Proud to be Black. Proud to look in the mirror and like what they see.

Give me back the key to my fate, the key to my determination. Please give me back the formula to a strong, loving and united Black family so we can grow up with more self-love, more love for each other, more trusting each other, more love for each other than we have for you. So we can stop trying to be like you and have more desire to be who we are, more desire to look like who we are. Flat nose, jet black face, sheep's wool hair. I like it. So we can be proud of jet-black skin, so we can be proud of kinky hair, so we can be proud of a flat nose.

So we can be proud. So we can be joyful. So we can be happy. So we can turn away from your greed, prejudice and hate. So we can turn more and more to love. Love, oh wonderful love. Love is the key. The key to the door of happiness. So leave me alone so I can love, so I can have peace and love, love, love.

I can be a proud, loving and strong Black male. Black baby, Black boy, and a proud and loving Black man.

You have taken away my ancestors' love and taught them to hate. Because you have fallen from grace, Mr. White Man, hell and not heaven is your fate.

Love and only love can unite you with me. Let yourself love and love will set us all free.

Self-Love or Self-Destruction

The Polarity of Feelings

*To every burst of laughter
There's some sadness undertow.*

*To every burst of anger
There's some pleasure trying to grow.*

Inside this book Asher explains the following:
- How we first possess lots of self-love
- How we lost it
- How can we work towards more self-love

Plus poems of inner feelings of sorrow, joy and happiness.

ISBN # 0-9636109-4-5